About the author

Sue Eckstein worked for VSO for many years in
London and the Gambia. Her plays include
The Tuesday Group, as well as *Kaffir Lilies*, *Laura*
and *Old School Ties* all for BBC Radio 4.
She lives in Brighton.

The
CLOTHS *of*
HEAVEN

Sue Eckstein

First published in 2009 by
Myriad Editions
59 Lansdowne Place
Brighton BN3 1FL

www.MyriadEditions.com

1 3 5 7 9 10 8 6 4 2

"He Wish ... *the Reeds* by Willi... Butler Yea... d with the p... ...ts.

A C... the

ISBN: 978-0-9549309-8-1

Printed on FSC-accredited paper by
CPI Antony Rowe, Chippenham, UK.

FSC
Mixed Sources
Product group from well-managed
forests and other controlled sources
Cert no. SGS-COC-2953
www.fsc.org
© 1996 Forest Stewardship Council

He Wishes for the Cloths of Heaven

W. B. Yeats

Had I the heavens' embroidered cloths,
Enwrought with golden and silver light,
The blue and the dim and the dark cloths
Of night and light and the half-light,
I would spread the cloths under your feet:
But I, being poor, have only my dreams;
I have spread my dreams under your feet;
Tread softly because you tread on my dreams.

For Alastair

Brighton, October 24th 1990

POST CARD

THE ADDRESS TO BE WRITTEN ON THIS SIDE

As promised, a post card.
I'd forgotten what an
English autumn could
be like – crisp and clear –
the sort of weather I used
to dream about in Bakinabe.
I've started making plans –
but I'm rather out of practice.
There's a good chance Guido
Ansaldi will take me on as a pupil in the Spring –
Rome seems a good place to be as any.
I think of you often. Look after yourself. R x

Daniel Maddison
FCO Tiokunda
C/O King Charles St
London SW1A 2AH

BAKINABE, WEST AFRICA, 1989

When Isabel Redmond walked out onto the veranda she could not help noticing that her husband's hands were firmly cupped round a pair of rather splendid black breasts.

"Thought you might like a cold drink, Patrick," she said with a cheery sigh, placing a tray with two glasses of lemonade on the only clear corner of a low wooden table.

"Ah Izzy, you're a marvel," said Patrick rather distractedly, as he carefully fastened the buttons of his companion's blouse, deftly giving one large, erect nipple a valedictory tweak as he tucked it in. "We'd just finished. Thirsty work, eh, Isatou?"

Isatou re-tied her headscarf and smiled her thanks as Isabel passed her a glass. Patrick, meanwhile, dismantled his tripod and put his cameras away with rather less enthusiasm and dexterity than he had demonstrated only moments earlier.

"Same time next week? Marvellous!" he said, ushering Isatou into the house and out of the front door.

Isabel picked up the empty glasses and put them down on the tray. She heard Patrick walk back along the corridor and into the shower room. She heard the rusty squeak as he turned on the shower, and the familiar sharp intake of breath as the cold water hit the top of his balding head. She looked out over the dusty road, the hedges of flaming bougainvillaea, the corrugated iron roofs and sighed again, this time slightly less cheerfully. Patrick. What was she to do with him? What could she do? As hobbies went, it was perhaps a little out of the ordinary but as a deviancy it was really quite mild.

It could be a lot worse. Decades in Africa had had a far more bizarre effect on many of the expatriates they had encountered over the years. What about Stanley Shea, that surveyor in Kaduna? The one Eleanor Cameron had known. Years ago now. It was one thing to shoot yourself in the head when your house-boy finally tired of your advances, but quite another to miss so badly that you spent the rest of your life in a nursing home in Worthing. And Thomas Kayne, that judge who had served in the colonial service and was now living out his retirement following a clan of Fulani herdsmen and their cattle as they roamed the Sahel. Rumour had it you could trace his journey by the pale-skinned, green-eyed children that peppered his route. And just what Father Seamus was doing up in Brikaba was anyone's guess.

Isabel looked down at the mess of papers and magazines on the table. Dusty back copies of *West Africa* and *Private Eye*, sheets of yellow paper covered in lines of poetry and crossings out. Recipes. Reminders. Letters. Bills. She shuffled them into ungainly piles. There should at least be a bit of order around the place.

Isabel had married Patrick when they were both still at Oxford and now, forty-one years, six children and two continents later, she could not imagine what life would be like without him. It would be strangely empty and devoid of any real meaning, despite her children, her teaching and her many other interests; none of them, admittedly, as exotic as Patrick's.

If Patrick ever thought about these things, which Isabel suspected he rarely did, he would have expressed very similar sentiments. Isabel was, quite literally, his better half, though he would have worked hard to think up a more erudite way of putting it. Every evening, except when one of their children was over from England or someone dropped in, they would walk, arm in arm, to six o'clock Mass at St Gabriel's and then stroll on to their favourite beachside bar. There they would sit beside each other in companionable silence, watching the sun go down, each with a cold beer and a well-worn novel or book of poetry. From time to time they would read out snippets that each thought the other would appreciate. Occasionally, Patrick would look around, smile wickedly, pull out a short blunt pencil from his top pocket and open his small black notebook.

Patrick went nowhere without this notebook, in which he would jot down snatches of overheard conversation and anything else that he thought might come in useful. There had been a bit of a commotion the previous month when one of his poems, 'Cocktails at Eight, Fenella', had appeared in the *London Review of Books*. It had just been bad timing that old Alec, the High Commissioner, had been on home leave when it came out, bad luck that his hosts had subscribed to it, and unfortunate that his wife, Fenella, in an uncharacteristically literary mood, had read it. Patrick and Isabel's relationship with the High Commission and the other British expatriates, at best tenuous, was now somewhat strained.

Isabel picked some dead flowers off the bougainvillaea and crunched up the brown petals. She held her hand over the veranda wall and watched as the dried fragments spun and eddied to the ground. It was so hot and so dry. You could taste the dust in your throat and feel it in your eyes. Isabel, who was not one to complain or to wish herself anywhere other than where she was, found herself longing for the rains. The roads would be a mess. Shoes – unworn for a couple of days – would be covered in a light dusting of mould, and you would drip with sweat all day and night. But the earth would yield the most marvellous treasures, and when the rain clouds cleared the sky would be an azure so deep that you thought you would weep with the beauty of it.

"Izzy, my love," said Patrick, coming onto the veranda, brandishing an airmail envelope in one hand and his reading glasses in the other, and dressed only in a towel, a pair of flip-flops and the canvas hat he was rarely seen without, "have you read this letter from Joe?" His large white stomach flopped comfortably over the towel.

"No. I was about to and then I got sidetracked. What does he have to say for himself?" Joe was their youngest child and only son. He had graduated in philosophy from Edinburgh University and, after a brief foray into journalism, had distressed both his parents by joining a merchant bank. As if that were not bad enough, he seemed to be doing remarkably well and appeared to have little interest in Africa except where it affected the commodities market.

"The bugger's fine," said Patrick affectionately, scanning the letter. "Moving in with Lucy, it seems."

"I hope she knows what she's letting herself in for," said Isabel who, while she adored her only son, disapproved of his cavalier attitude towards his girlfriends and life in general. "She seems far too good for him. I hope she doesn't let him walk all over her." Isabel felt herself to be partially to blame for what she saw as Joe's shortcomings. A much longed-for son and brother, tall, blond and beautiful, he had spent his youth at a Catholic boys' boarding school inconveniently set in the middle of several hundred acres of Yorkshire dale. When he left, he was like a lion released back into the wild. Girls were the zebras he had always known were out there (he had five sisters, after all) but had rarely had the chance to pounce upon. Isabel had failed to find the equivalent of a tranquilliser dart with which to curb his enthusiasm and Patrick had not been much help, openly enjoying Joe's tales of conquest.

"Seems Lucy's cousin is out here. At the High Commission," continued Patrick. "Some kind of second secretary. Poor sod."

"That must be Daniel Maddison," said Isabel. "He's that slim, dark-haired chap who arrived a couple of months ago. Only about twenty-five or so. I bumped into him in the supermarket – quite literally – and we got talking – a few weeks ago now. I remember telling you at the time. He seemed very pleasant, if a little disappointed."

"Why? Not enough cheddar cheese and Branston pickle for him?"

"Quite the opposite, I think. He seemed amazed that there was so much imported stuff available. I think he imagined he was being posted into the bush or something."

"Probably read too much Graham Greene. It does that to you. Still, if he can read at all it singles him out from the rest of the diplomatic crowd," said Patrick contemptuously.

"And I saw him again in town last week," said Isabel,

frowning as she recalled the occasion. "I don't think he saw me. He was standing outside one of those Lebanese cloth shops, staring in at the piles of batik print. He looked a bit odd, actually."

"What do you mean, odd?" asked Patrick.

"I don't know. Sort of distracted. Confused. That sort of thing. He looked as though he was about to go in, and then suddenly he turned away and walked off."

"Probably overpowered by the vulgarity of the colours," said Patrick dismissively. "Not quite the right thing for those High Commission cocktail parties, are they?"

"Oh, Patrick, don't be such a beast. I think we should invite him round. Especially if he's Lucy's cousin. You never know, she may survive life with our angelic son for more than the usual six months. And anyway, he seems interesting."

"Why? Because he has a thing about garish material and a passing interest in Africa?"

"You're just jealous, Patrick, in case you have a rival for the position of resident iconoclast. I'm going to drop him a note and suggest he joins us for a drink. So there. Now go on, you old goat. Get dressed. Mass starts in twenty minutes."

Isabel took the letter with one hand and Patrick's glasses with the other and then hesitated. Dropping them onto the table, she stepped forward and wrapped her arms around him. His arms enveloped her and, as they did so, his towel dropped to the floor. He buried his face in her hair and nuzzled her ear. She felt the hairs on the back of her neck bristle.

"What about eight o'clock Mass instead?" they said

together, laughing as they walked hand in hand into their bedroom, the damp towel trailing behind them.

Daniel Maddison had offered to join the High Commissioner on his visit to Juntaur. He needed an excuse to get off the High Commission compound. Maybe a trip down the coast would clear his head.

The journey had started inauspiciously with old Alec snapping at the driver – something to do with the angle of the Union Jack on the bonnet – and then going into a sulky decline in the back of the Range Rover. He had responded to Daniel's enthusiastic commentary first with irritable grunts and then with a moody silence. Two hours into the journey and old Alec's temper was showing no sign of improving.

The road skirted the fish-smoking huts and the smell of barbecued fish caught the back of Daniel's throat. Every now and then, groups of small children would run out of their compounds, shouting *Toubab! Toubab!*, laughing, and trying to touch the side of the car as it sped by. Daniel gazed out of the window, smiling to himself. Where else could you spend a working day driving down palm-fringed dirt roads, with the sea shimmering behind the dunes, past wizened old men sitting on wooden benches in doorways watching the world go by and groups of women carrying water pots on their heads, their hips swaying in ways which made it difficult for him to swallow. Go on. Where else? Where else, for that matter, would you get fish called *bonga*?

Daniel felt himself relax. The unease he had been experiencing over the past few weeks seemed to be diminishing. But if he shut his eyes for a moment he could still see her face. Pale and still, her fair hair falling over her eyes as she bent over the rolls of cloth.

Daniel glanced sideways at the High Commissioner and noticed that he had tired of staring at the back of the driver's head and was now immersed in a thick novel with a scarlet and gold-embossed cover. Well at least he was spared the ordeal of having to make conversation with Alec, who appeared to regard him as only slightly less strange than the people he insisted on calling "the natives" whenever he felt it was safe to do so. Daniel shuddered as he recalled the last conversation they had had while waiting for a visiting dignitary at the airport:

"Got a girlfriend back home then?"

"I'm sorry?"

"A girlfriend. You know. Two legs, a pair of t—"

"Yes – I know what you—"

"Good-looking chap like you. Must have them queuing up."

"Well …"

"What about Hélène?"

"Hélène who?"

"Smets. Hélène Smets."

"She's married."

Daniel could still see the look that Alec had given him – a combination of undisguised incredulity and amusement.

The driver turned sharply off the main road and drove into the village chief's compound, the little Union Jack flapping through clouds of yellow dust. Old Alec snapped his book shut. The muffled sound of children calling out grew louder and louder. Hands waved, inches from their faces; grimy fingers tapped on the glass and doors. They stepped from the car. The heat and uninsulated shrieks of laughter hit them. Daniel stood back and watched as Alec gasped and clutched the bonnet and tried, without success, to find his handkerchief in one of the many pockets of his tropical-weight beige suit. Alec and Daniel were engulfed by a group of men in long blue or white robes, all reaching for their hands and greeting them. They were led to a wooden bench outside a building so new it seemed as though the bricks could be lifted from their soft bed of cement. Alec looked, to Daniel, as though he was gearing up for an afternoon in the dentist's chair. The village chief thanked them, in a mixture of broken English and Bakawa, for the generous gift, the fruits of which they were obviously sitting in front of. A pair of scissors was handed to Alec. He cut the yellow ribbon. A huge cheer went up.

Daniel noticed that the High Commissioner was wiping his hands on the back of his jacket, probably hoping no one would see. If he would just relax, keep his hair on. What little there was left of it. It wouldn't have taken much for him to just cut the piece of ribbon with a smile, declare the community centre open with a bit of good grace and a couple of words of encouragement, would it? Why couldn't he just try to enjoy it? Listen to the drums? Look at the women beginning to dance?

First one woman then two, then ten, twenty, shuffled in thin plastic flip-flops to the sandy space in front of the building. Several had sleeping babies tied tightly to their backs. The infants' heads wobbled and shook as they slept. The women danced wildly to the drum beats. The whole space was a mass of movement and colour as they clapped and turned.

Old Alec was squinting at his watch, wiping rivulets

of sweat from his eyes. The sun was directly overhead now. He should have worn a hat, thought Daniel. *Alec Moss, who died of sunstroke just three years before he was due to retire from the Foreign Office, will be remembered for his uncanny ability to absent himself, in spirit, if not in person, from any situation in which he did not feel comfortable. Rarely seen without a large gin and tonic in one hand and a pretty girl in the other, Alec Moss will be much missed by his wife Fenella, Isatou in the visa office, Mariatou at the supermarket, Fatou at the British Council library, Yassin at the ...*

All around Daniel, the men were chewing kola nuts. His neighbours spat great gobs of red saliva onto the ground and laughed. A group of men were crouched over a charcoal stove, brewing up *ataaya*. They emptied cones of white sugar into boiling green tea then poured the frothing brown liquid into small glasses. They tipped the tea from glass to glass, holding the glasses far apart. The waterfall of tea glinted in the sun.

Daniel's eyes wandered over to where a young woman was feeding her baby. Her eyes were like chocolate wells. They stared back impassively. The baby, saturated with milk, flopped off the nipple, mouth open, eyes shut. Its tiny black toes curled and uncurled. The breast shone with milk and saliva.

There was a huff of irritation at his ear. Old Alec was stamping and rolling his eyes like some kind of demented horse. A demented sweaty horse with a cocktail party to go to. The driver, who had ambled over, drawn by the smell of food it now appeared certain he was not going to get, muttered something in Bakawa. The village chief laughed and slapped him on the back in sympathy.

Daniel, reluctant to leave without eating the meal that had been so carefully prepared in their honour, shook hands with as many villagers as he could, then opened the car door. It was like an oven in there. Alec was already sitting in the back seat, fiddling with the buttons of his jacket. Daniel got in next to him. The driver turned the key in the ignition, jabbed on the air conditioning, and screeched away in a cloud of dust and disappointment.

High above him, a vulture circles. Thomas Kayne squints into the sky, his green eyes disappearing into creases of leathery brown skin. What is it? He is losing the words. They dance in his head, forming pairs, couplets, coming together, parting again. There are moments of clarity when the words line up in the right language, in the right order. Moments of calm in the heaving, twirling dance hall of his mind.

The words are playing with him now, darting this way and that. He is reminded of a. A what? Sharp, blue, quick, smelly-nested, black what – black beak. Black sheep. Baa Baa Black Sheep Have You Any Words? The Wool Sack. Good King Richard. Kingfisher. Stop. Shining-Blue Kingfisher. *Alcedo quadribrachys*. Hold on to those words. But the bird – that's the word – bird. The bird in the sky – what is that? That's not a king, a king what? King Onigbogi of Benin. The Alafin of Oyo. Alafin, Elephant. I wish to make a trunk call. Trunk Trunk Humpety Hump. There used to be camel trains here, you know. Last train for Beckenham. Hurry along, young man, we haven't got all day. She'll be waiting for you, you know. Pretty girl that Eleanor. I'd snap her up if I were you. Hazy days, lazy ways. Bring on the dancing words. Journey out here all right? You must need a drink. What's your tipple, then? Damned hot today, eh, Tom? Fetch the master a drink, Musa Mohammed, Mohammed Musa, Musa Musa that's no excusa. Polly put the kettle on. Polly *cholli jigawal*.

Jigawal. Vulture. *Cholli*. Bird. Thomas Kayne smiles and lifts a quivering hand high above his head into the pale clear sky, as if to grasp the words and hold them tight in his fist. Around him, the thin goats graze. The young herdsmen walk slowly amongst them. They hook their arms over the long wooden sticks that rest on their shoulders. Their wide-brimmed leather hats shade them from the glare of the sun.

A piece of green plastic bag drifts towards Thomas Kayne. A goat stops to nibble it. Kayne remembers something. Something small and green. What? A green frog. A frog prince. A tree frog. A fat hog. Home again, home again, jiggedy jog. Roast the hog. Cook the books. Yes. A small green phrase book. *Taylor's Fulani-Hausa Phrase-Book*, 1926. The sentences line up for inspection.

The merchandise that comes from the north consists of ivory and ostrich feathers.

Before the white man came there was much strife and highway robbery.

The labourers to clear your compound passed here a little while ago.

Take this hobbling rope and hobble the horse fore and hind.

I shall issue new putties and cummerbunds tomorrow.

Thomas Kayne swirls the phrases round in his mouth, tasting each syllable with his tongue. As they fade, they leave a bitter aftertaste. He brushes his wild grey hair from his face. *Min njokki kakadi lawol ngol*, he says quietly. We have come to the end of this road.

A warm breeze wafted over the garden, bringing with it the sound of the waves and the smell of frangipani. Strings of fairy lights swayed between the trees. The flag, Daniel noticed with a smile that verged on the sardonic, was flying. From the veranda came the usual sounds of ice chinking against glasses, the low hum of conversation punctuated by the odd familiar hoot of laughter. So Fenella was up and about again, then. Amazing how quickly the High Commissioner's wife recovered from malaria. Must be all the quinine in the tonic water. Its restorative powers seemed to have worked for Alec too, who appeared to be deeply engrossed in conversation with the Togolese Ambassador's wife.

Daniel approached the drinks table and noticed that Baboucar the garden boy had been appropriated as barman. No longer dressed in his loose blue robes, he was immaculate in white shirt and trousers. Unused to the constraint, he was fiddling with his flies in a way that would have been alarming in any other situation.

"Baboucar! *Salaamalekum*."

"*Malekumsalaam*, Mr Daniel." Baboucar grinned from ear to ear and held up a bottle of gin with a flourish.

"You look great! Like the trousers. I'll have a whisky, thanks. No ice. How are the children, and Bintas One and Two?"

"They are all well, Mr Daniel. Binta One is gone up-country. Her father, he is very sick."

Baboucar was devoted to his two wives, who shared the same name and the same good looks, and lived with him in the small hut at the back of the compound. Between them they had seven children, of whom Daniel had grown quite fond since his arrival at the High Commission. Baboucar took a tall tumbler and poured the whisky up to the brim.

"Erm, Baboucar. Not full. Just a little," suggested Daniel, checking that Fenella was not anywhere near. She had been known to get rid of staff for far less. He remembered with a shudder the incident involving Mariama and Fenella's shih-tzu. Mariama had only been trying to be helpful by cutting the smelly dog's fringe so that it could see.

"Tip it back in. Look, I'll do it. There, that's fine. NO! No tonic, thanks. Not with this drink."

"No tonic, Mr Daniel?" asked Baboucar with wonder. "Only this little?"

"Yes, that's lovely. Just remember. Whisky – no tonic and not full tumbler, not in public anyway."

"OK, Mr Daniel. No problem. Thank you," said Baboucar, no doubt relieved he would not be having to break the bad news about an imminent move to Binta Two, who, though the younger and second wife, when roused reminded Baboucar uncomfortably of Madam High Commissioner.

Daniel looked over at the crowd by the house. For a moment he thought he saw her – that fair hair, those strange, sad eyes. But she would hardly be here, at a High Commission drinks party, would she? He found himself smiling at the unlikely image of the silent, sombre woman chattering away with a crowd of expatriates and ambassadors and a smattering of old Alec's "favourite natives", plucking canapés from circulating silver trays.

No, it could not have been her. Anyway, now was scarcely the time to try to work on that conundrum. There was mingling to be done. He took a deep breath.

"Here goes. Into the bloody lions' den," he muttered grimly, taking a large swig of whisky.

"Lions? I didn't know there was big game here. It gets better and better."

Daniel looked up from his glass and found himself a little too close to a short, stocky man with rather unpleasant teeth. He recognised the south London vowels but not the speaker. The man was holding out a hand expectantly.

Oh, Christ! No! Why me? thought Daniel. He shut his eyes for a second or two. A vision of a phone box, a flash of red tights and a sudden escape flashed through his mind. Then he opened his eyes and held out his hand.

"Daniel Maddison. Aid Attaché. How do you do?"

"AIDS Attaché. Blimey! I didn't know it was that bad! What do you do? Go round with an attaché bag handing out condoms?" The little man guffawed. A glob of saliva landed on Daniel's tie. I am not paid enough for this job, thought Daniel, gazing at the man with a fixed smile. The man took a drag on his cigarette, blew out a cloud of smoke that enveloped them both, coughed, and came a step nearer Daniel.

"Keeps the mozzies away, you know," he whispered conspiratorially. Daniel held his breath as a wave of nicotine, gin and halitosis swept over him.

"Bob Newpin. New Pin Enterprises. 'Timeshares for those with times to share.' Neat, eh? Here, I've got a card somewhere. Cast your eyes over this." Newpin thrust a rather sweaty card literally under Daniel's nose.

"Thank you," said Daniel, glancing at it and taking a step backwards. "You're here on business, I take it?"

"Too right I am. Place is a gold mine. Sun, sea, sand and a bit of the other I shouldn't wonder. Had a meeting with the Minister of Tourism this morning. Should be a piece of cake. I've heard you can oil his palm for the price of a weekend's shopping in Croydon."

Daniel shuddered, visualising lengthy correspondence with Prisoners Abroad, calls to a distraught wife in Eltham, letters from MPs, the works. Why these morons thought they could come over here and pollute everything with their foul get-rich-quick schemes, he just could not understand.

Newpin was waving his cigarette around as he talked. There was a stench of singed hair. Daniel put his hand up to his head and fingered the frizzled ends. Newpin, oblivious of his incendiary activities, continued. He was clearly not on his first, or even second, double gin. "Miles of golden beaches, half-naked ladies selling mangoes as big as tits, beach boys with rippling muscles for those who incline towards a bit of black, if you know what I mean. I've half a mind to settle here myself."

Daniel's grip tightened on his tumbler. Would smashing a glass into the head of a guest at a High Commission cocktail party constitute an international incident? Would he be protected by diplomatic immunity? Christ! What was happening to him? He was sure he had never harboured murderous thoughts before he came out here.

Newpin dropped his cigarette end and ground it into the lawn. "Called in to leave my card with the First Secretary, Commerce, here at the Embassy and before you know it, here I am. Invited to a blooming do." He paused to get out another Rothmans and light it with a shiny metal lighter.

"High Commission," said Daniel.

"Yeah, whatever." Newpin dragged heavily on his cigarette and blew another cloud of smoke into Daniel's eyes. "Anyway," he said, swaying rather alarmingly and raising his glass, which now contained only a couple of pieces of ice floating in some rather scummy dregs, "Here's to shared times, times shared, big times, big bucks and big tits. Cheers, Damian."

"Daniel," said Daniel grimly. "Cheers." He turned away from Newpin and started towards the veranda again. Then he stopped. No, he was not going in. He had had enough for one night. Another bloody mindless conversation and he did not know what he might be capable of. Any more of Fenella's "do" and it would be his mother writing to Prisoners Abroad. He headed back to the drinks table. He smiled at the garden boy turned barman and held out his glass.

"Fill it to the top, Baboucar."

"But Mr Daniel. Did you not say only a little of whisky in a glass?"

"That was before, Baboucar. This is after. Go on. Just this once."

Baboucar smiled and shook his head wonderingly as he poured the amber liquid to the rim of the glass. *Toubabs!* Even that nice Mr Daniel. You could never really understand what they meant.

Daniel sipped off the top centimetre of whisky. "Cheers, Baboucar. See you. Here, buy something nice for those children of yours." He thrust some coins into

Baboucar's hand, turned, and walked swiftly away from the house and into the darkness.

A few yards beyond the high wrought-iron gates and sentry box, Daniel stopped. He realised that he had no idea where he was going, apart from in the opposite direction from the cocktail party. He looked round and saw the guard watching him quizzically. Daniel waved at him – somewhat hindered by the fact that he was still clutching a tumbler full of whisky – and turned back to the road, striding purposefully towards nowhere in particular.

He felt a curious kind of elation as he walked, avoiding the storm drains and potholes and giving a wide berth to the street dogs that roamed in scrawny, companionable packs. A sudden breeze brought with it the smell of sewage, honeysuckle blossom and cheap tobacco. He realised, to his surprise, that this was the first time since he had arrived that he had walked anywhere after dark. He listened to the night. Beyond the whirr of generators and the low muttering of the watchmen as they squatted in twos or threes outside high walls and gates, brewing up *ataaya* and puffing on cheroots, all he could hear was the sound of the sea and the scuff of his shoes in the sand as he walked.

The road led towards the tourist hotel complexes. The guests would be sitting in the air-conditioned, stripped pine restaurants and bars, eating pizza and chips and drinking imported lager, free for a few hours of the touts selling them fruit and batik skirts and shirts on the beach. They were an extraordinary lot. Only a couple of weeks ago, while he had been talking to the wife of that British Council person in the supermarket

– what was her name? Imogen or something like that – a Swedish woman wearing nothing but a thong and a deep tan had asked one of the shelf stackers if they had any tinned mangoes. It was as though most of the tourists' sense of perspective and sensitivity had somehow missed the plane in Luton or Stockholm or Hamburg and was waiting to be reunited at some later date.

Daniel remembered with some embarrassment that Isabel – yes that was her name – had just raised an eyebrow and continued their conversation undeterred, while he had been unable to say anything at all until the mahogany buttocks had disappeared behind a stack of Libby's Pineapple Chunks. Even then, all he had done was mutter something pathetic about the unexpected availability of incongruous imported goods.

His thoughts were interrupted by the sound of a vehicle heading towards him at speed. He stepped back into a bougainvillaea hedge and out of the glare of the headlights. The car passed, sending up waves of sand and grit, then stopped with a sudden screech of brakes about fifty yards up the road. Daniel could see the outline of two people – a man and a woman – sitting in the front seats. He was emerging from the hedge when he saw the man raise a fist into the air. Daniel winced and turned his head away as it came down. When he opened his eyes, he saw that it had crashed down onto the dashboard. He could hear muffled shouting, first a man's voice, then a woman's. The passenger door opened and the woman got out. The man leaned over the seat towards her as the door slammed in his face.

"Walk then!" His furious voice pierced the darkness. He smashed both hands onto the steering wheel, started the engine, and drove off, horn blasting. Daniel watched from the shelter of the hedge.

"Are you all right?" a familiar voice called from behind him. He was about to reply, when he realised that the question was not addressed to him. Isabel Redmond had emerged from her gate. "Only I heard the shouting. And you seem to be without transport now. Can I give you a lift somewhere?"

There was a pause and the woman turned and called out, "No, I'm fine. Thanks." She paused again and brushed the hair off her face. "I don't live far away."

Daniel recognised the fair, wavy hair and the way that she pushed it away from her face, up off her forehead.

"Are you sure? I'll happily come with you."

"I'm sure. Really. Thank you. I'm sorry for disturbing you."

Isabel stood for a few moments watching the woman walk away, then turned back towards the gate.

"Good gracious! What are you doing here?"

"Hello. Isabel, isn't it? I'm Daniel from the High Commission."

"Yes, I know what you are in the Foreign Office hierarchy. I mean what are you doing in my hedge? Did you have anything to do with that scene out there?"

"God, no! I was just out walking when the car passed. I was trying to get out of its way. They didn't see me. I would've done something. I mean, if you hadn't come out."

But was that really true, he wondered. In times of crisis, when had he ever done anything other than wince and look away?

"I doubt there is much you could have done. I wish

she had let me take her home, though. I wonder who she is?"

"She works at the Lebanese cloth warehouse on Canal Street."

Isabel gave him a curious look.

"Why don't you come in for a drink? I could do with one, and there are at least six flies in whatever it is you have in that glass. I'm sure Patrick would like to meet you. We know someone in common. You're Lucy Maddison's cousin, aren't you?"

"I am. How do you know that?"

"She has the misfortune of being our son's latest girlfriend."

"So you're Joe's mother? I've heard a lot about him. Well, he's very lucky. She's great, Lucy. The two of us used to spend summers with our very adventurous great-aunt Eleanor in Oxford."

"Not Eleanor Cameron by any chance?"

"Yes. Why?"

"We knew her when we were in Borno State – on our first posting. Must be nearly forty years ago. Well, isn't it a small world? How is she?"

"She's very well, I think. Still busy with various committees and things to do with West Africa. Threatening to visit me next dry season."

"Well, do remember us to her next time you're in touch," Isabel continued as she ushered him through the gate and up the path to the house.

As they walked onto the veranda, Patrick Redmond put down his book, adjusted the piece of cloth he was wearing as a sarong and raised his grubby canvas hat.

"Ah! Our Man in Havana, I see. So we meet at last.

How do you do? Here, sit down. Aren't you meant to be at some High Commission event?" Patrick waved his hand vaguely in the direction of an embossed invitation on the bookshelf. "Thought I'd give it a miss, myself. Though I imagine the crème of the expatriate set are, even as I speak, gathered round the piano singing early Barry Manilow. What do you think?"

"Yes, well …"

"Oh, Paddy, just give the boy a drink, for goodness' sake, not an interrogation."

"I was just enquiring—"

"Well, don't. Daniel – a beer?" Isabel asked, taking the tumbler from his hand and disappearing into the kitchen.

"Yes, please. That would be great."

"What was all that racket outside?" asked Patrick.

"Some kind of domestic argument, I think."

"Local girl?"

"No, English. Sounded it, at least."

Isabel came onto the veranda with the drinks. "I hope she'll be all right. It's so hard to know what to do in these situations," she said.

"Maybe our Honorary Consul here should keep an eye on her," said Patrick, winking at Daniel.

Isabel looked at him kindly and then at Patrick, less so. "I'm sure he will," she said in a tone that suggested a different topic would be in order. Patrick looked at her quizzically, opened his mouth and thought better of it. "How are they all, then, up at the nerve centre?" he asked while flicking through his book. "Old Alec and Fenella and the delightfully endowed Isatou?"

"Fine, thank you."

"How are you settling in, Daniel?" asked Isabel quickly. "Do you like it here?"

"I love it. Here, I mean. Not the job particularly, though it has its moments. Sometimes," he added lamely as he thought of his recent encounter with Bob Newpin. "I've wanted to live in West Africa ever since I can remember."

Patrick looked up from his book.

"I had relatives in the Colonial Service – I was just telling Isabel about my great-aunt Eleanor – so it's always been there, in the background," Daniel continued. "It's hard to describe. There's something about the people and the movement and the smells. There's a vibrancy that—"

"Izzy, our Burnt-Out Case is clearly not quite. More beers all round, I think."

Two hours later, Daniel rose to leave, swaying slightly. Isabel kissed him warmly on the cheek.

"Join us for a sundowner any evening. We're usually at Bakari's on the beach," she said, steering him towards the door.

"Yes, do. I won't get up," Patrick added.

"Can't, more like it, you old soak. Safe journey home, Daniel."

Brighton, March 14th 1991

POST CARD

THE ADDRESS TO BE WRITTEN ON THIS SIDE

Spring in Rome didn't work
out in the end for various
reasons that I will tell you
about one day — but there
are compensations and
there is always next year.
How strange it feels to look
ahead with optimism.
I hope you can too.
If anyone deserves a good life, it is you. R x

Daniel Maddison
FCO Tiasunda
c/o King Charles St
London SW1A2AH

Fenella lay on the bed in her bra and pants, smoking and leafing through an old copy of *Vogue*. The years, and a rather good Harley Street practitioner, had been kind to her and, though she said it herself, she was looking pretty good for fifty-seven. From time to time, she lifted her eyes from the magazine and inspected her smoothly tanned legs for stray hairs and cellulite. No. She could not complain, and neither could Paavo Valjakka at the Finnish Embassy.

From the en suite bathroom came the sound of singing and the occasional fart. Fenella rolled her eyes to the ceiling and saw herself reflected in a large mirror. Their predecessors had had something of a reputation. She had always meant to have it taken down, but somehow never got round to it.

"Hurry up, Alec. What are you doing in there?"

"What do you think I'm doing? Having tea with the Princess Royal? Can't a man have a crap in peace?"

"Not for half an hour, he can't."

"Half an hour? Hardly! And while we're talking about keeping people waiting, you didn't exactly seem to be in a hurry to leave tonight."

"It wasn't a question of leaving. It was our party."

"Well, calling it a day then."

"What, and leave those VSO volunteers alone with the beer?"

"They'd have gone eventually and ..." The rest of Alec's sentence was drowned by the sound of the lavatory flushing.

"What? I wish you wouldn't do that," called Fenella irritably.

"Do what?"

"Drone on and on when I can't hear you."

"It wasn't anything important," said Alec, his mouth full of foaming toothpaste.

"Really? You surprise me!"

Alec spat loudly, then walked into the bedroom, nonchalantly scratching his scrotum. Fenella blew out a cloud of smoke and looked at him with an expression of benign revulsion. She stubbed out the cigarette, drained the rest of her gin and tonic and went into the bathroom. Alec put on his pyjamas, and climbed into bed. He reached for his Jeffrey Archer novel and reading glasses. A few grains of sand that had become caught between the pages fell out onto the sheets. He brushed them to the floor, wondering how they had got there, then shuddered as he recalled the trip to Juntaur. Had that really only been earlier today? Still, that was it for this year as far as visiting the natives in their natural surroundings went. He thought, briefly, of Bunny Fellowes in Berlin and Freddy Reeves in Paris and sighed.

Fenella, in apricot satin nightdress and Clarins Rejuvenating Night Cream, got into bed beside him.

"Danny boy disappeared early," she said, plumping her pillows before propping herself up to light a last cigarette.

"Probably off looking for some totty. You should have seen the way he was staring at those local girls' bosoms today."

"I thought he was a left footer."

"A Catholic? No. I'm sure he's C of E. He was a choral scholar at Christchurch."

"No, not a Catholic. A poofter. You know."

"Catholics aren't all poofters, though come to think

of it, those priests …"

"Forget about Catholics, Alec."

"Well, why did you bring them up in the first place?"

"I didn't. You did."

"It was definitely you, Fenella."

"Just forget it, OK? I meant queer."

"Well why didn't you say that in the first place?"

"I did, actually."

Fenella turned her back to her husband, spreading ash across the pillow as she did so. If Alec wasn't quite so dim, she thought, they might be strolling along the Champs-Élysées now, instead of sweating it out in this godforsaken hole. She could just imagine Cynthia Reeves, squeezed into a little Chanel number, sipping champagne at the Bristol Hotel. The nearest she got to Parisian glamour here was the occasional bottle of duty free Rive Gauche.

"What makes you think Daniel's queer, then?" asked Alec, leaning over her. She grimaced as she felt his hot breath on her left shoulder.

"It's obvious, isn't it?"

"Not to me it isn't, or I wouldn't have asked, would I?"

"Well, for a start, he's a very natty dresser. His socks even match his ties."

"I hardly think that's a sign of rampant homosexuality."

"And he's always so damned pleasant to everyone."

"You might find pleasantness unnatural, Fenella, but it's not necessarily —"

"And then there's that secret handshake."

"Secret handshake? So that's how they work out who's going into a public toilet for a wee and who's going for a quick—"

"I was joking, Alec."

"Oh." Alec sounded disappointed. "Well, anyway, I'm sure he's not."

"At least that ghastly Redmond couple didn't turn up," she said, stubbing out her cigarette on the inside rim of her empty glass.

"I don't think they'd have had the gall, after that poetry business."

"That dreadful dumpy woman. Talk about letting yourself go. And that filthy hat of his. I'm surprised they can bear to look at each other."

Alec, emboldened by this rare moment of accord, placed a hand on his wife's stomach. His fingers started feeling their way down.

"For goodness' sake, Alec," she snapped. "What do you think you're doing?"

"I just thought—"

"Well, don't." She switched off the light.

"Goodnight, then?"

"Goodnight, Alec."

"You're sure you're not in the mood for—"

"Absolutely sure."

Alec lay in the dark, listening as his wife's breathing became quieter and more regular. It was lucky, really, he thought, that Fenella had developed an interest in bridge and even luckier that she had to go over to the Finnish Embassy on the other side of town to play it. Reaching down inside his pyjama bottoms, he looked up at the mirror. As his hand moved, he could see the reflection of Isatou's voluptuous black buttocks pumping up and down, up and down, up and down. Alec's smile widened; his eyes opened and then shut in an exquisite grimace.

"For Christ's sake, Alec," muttered Fenella in her sleep, yanking the sheets towards her.

Alec lay quietly gasping. Then he wiped his hand very carefully on the back of her nightdress, turned over and went to sleep.

Daniel squeezed his way along the narrow paths of the market, his face brushing against the warm round backs of babies tied tightly to the women who strolled between the stalls, balancing containers of cooking oil, or flimsy red and white striped plastic bags of vegetables, on their heads. He breathed in the milky, tinny smell of the sleeping babies, the odour of rotting cabbage and kola nut spittle mingled with smoked fish and musty rice.

"Come here, sir – nice things."

"Bananas – very cheap – come, come."

"Any pens? Any bonbons?"

"New videos, no pirates, come, buy."

"Give me one lamasi ..."

The shouts of traders competing for business, the sound of raised voices bargaining over clusters of misshapen tomatoes, the music of Bob Marley and Salif Keita blaring from the cassette-copying booths fought for space in the hot dry air. As Daniel took off his sunglasses to wipe his face, the market exploded into colour. Gleaming aluminium cooking pots and gaudy Chinese enamelware flashed in the sun, piles of aubergines glowed in a purple haze, pyramids of tinned tomato paste glinted. The cloth of the women's robes and headdresses dazzled him.

He found himself walking to the edge of the market, towards the fetid canal which flowed, sluggishly, to the port. Here the rickety kiosks selling batteries, cigarettes, and sticks of white bread gave way to larger shops, cloth warehouses and wholesalers. The vast concrete buildings stretched back from the litter-strewn, potholed pavements.

Daniel stopped outside the largest cloth shop, hesitated for a moment, then ducked under the raised grille and went in. He blinked, unable to make out anything until his eyes became accustomed to the dark interior. Fans turned above the high wooden shelves and ankle-height platforms that held the cloth. Motes of dust danced in the few rays of sun that had penetrated the half-closed shutters. The floor was concrete; bare light bulbs hung from the high ceiling. There was a tall wooden desk and chair in the corner, of the kind favoured by Dickensian bookkeepers. On top of the desk he noticed a calculator, a pile of receipts on a spike, and a novel spread face down, bursting from its spine.

He walked along the aisles, trailing his fingers across the bolts of cloth. As he did so, he could feel the textures in his teeth and on his tongue: the smooth damasks, the fuzzy appliqués, the stiff nets, the deep mauve gauze dotted with pink felt, the gold-embossed rayon trickling strands of silver thread, the lemon polyester with its universe of sparkling orange stars.

He became aware of the hum of a computer and looked up. At the far end of the shop was a glass-fronted gallery. A window had been slid open and he could hear the high-pitched whine of a fax machine. He could just make out the dark head of someone sitting in front of the computer.

He walked back along the first aisle, then stopped suddenly by one of the thick concrete columns. She was sitting at the high wooden desk, bent over the book. He wondered how she had got there without his noticing. It was the closest he had been to her. Daniel could see traces of perspiration on her forehead. From time to time, she raised a hand to push her damp hair from her face. She was wearing a simple black cotton dress. Her thin arms were bare.

"Rachel!"

She held her place in the book with a finger and looked up at the gallery.

Daniel felt his palms prick with sweat. Rachel. Surely that couldn't just be another of those coincidences?

"Rachel. Did you hear me? Has that consignment from China arrived?"

"Not yet."

"I'm going out for a while. Deal with it when it comes, will you?"

She turned back to her book without replying.

A short, dark, immaculately dressed man walked down the wooden stairs from the gallery. He stopped by the desk, gripped her arm with one hand and turned her face to his with the other. He kissed her slowly on the lips, then let her go.

"Faysal and Suhad are coming for dinner, darling. Please be ready," he called behind him as he left.

She wiped her mouth on the back of her hand, then flicked through the book until she found her place.

Daniel hesitated a moment, then went up to the desk. He could see the imprint of the man's fingers on her arm. He took a deep breath.

"You like Mervyn Peake, then?"

She looked up and stared at him impassively for a few seconds before returning to the book.

"I loved the first two Gormenghast books …"

Daniel stopped, unnerved by the lack of response. He felt himself blush. He could kick himself. Not only did he do a good line in wincing and looking away, he could come up with a damn fine irrelevant question.

"I've seen you a few times, here in the shop."

"I know," she said, without lifting her eyes from the book.

"I hope you don't think I'm—"

"Do you want to buy some cloth?" She shut the book and stared at him.

"Sorry?"

"Do you want to buy some cloth? If not, I suggest—"

"Yes, I do." Daniel scanned the rows, his eyes frantic. "Some of the – the damask – that bright pink. The one with the fuchsia pattern in it. Three metres."

She walked to the bolt of cloth with an elegant weariness, leaving her leather sandals under the desk. He watched her as she dragged the bolt onto a long wooden table, measured it with a wooden ruler, snipped it with a pair of large black scissors, and then ripped the piece from the bolt. She folded the cloth, wrapped it in paper, tied the parcel with string, and handed it to him.

"That's forty lamasi. Thanks. Any more? You're obviously quite a connoisseur. What about the crimson and purple nylon over there? Or the pure cotton with repeating images of Pope John Paul II?" Her voice was icily polite.

"No. Thanks. This is fine. I'm sorry to have—"

"The Virgin Mary on best quality polyester?" She pulled out length after length of cloth. "We've got the Wailers around here somewhere, too. On rayon."

"No. This is great. Look, if I've—"

"Ethnic African batik? Freshly imported from the Netherlands."

"No, really. This is just what I wanted."

"No it isn't."

"No. You're right. I just wondered who you are."

"Who I am?"

"And what you're doing here."

"What does it look like?" She returned to her chair and opened the book again.

"And I wanted to see if you were all right."

"Why shouldn't I be?"

"After last night."

She looked up at him. Her eyes were greyish-green, he noticed.

"I saw you and – and him," Daniel nodded up at the gallery, "on the coast road. Last night. I just wondered—"

"I'm fine," said Rachel flatly. She took a deep breath. "But thanks for asking."

"That's OK. It's just that things seemed, sort of, well, difficult. Look, I'll give you my card. Perhaps you'd give me a ring sometime. If I can do anything."

She looked at the card. "Yes. Thanks. I may do that. Sometime."

"Well, thanks for this," said Daniel, as he picked up his parcel. "Goodbye."

He walked back out into the street and watched Rachel for a moment through the grille. He saw her look at the card again, then slowly rip it up and let the tiny pieces flutter to the floor.

Barbara Maddison shakes the rain from her umbrella and rings the bell. November. There is probably no more miserable time of year. Except perhaps February. She watches through the frosted glass as her elderly aunt walks slowly up the corridor and opens the door.

"Barbara!" the old woman exclaims, undoing the chain. "How lovely to see you. Come in."

"Sorry for coming without any warning, Aunt Eleanor," says Barbara, taking off her wet coat and wiping her boots on the mat. "But I was at an Amnesty meeting in Witney and it seemed daft not to drop in. How are you?"

"Fine. A bit stiff in the mornings."

"How's that new hip performing?" asks Barbara, catching sight of herself in the hall mirror and grimacing at her dishevelled reflection.

"Better than the original, I can tell you. Roll on hip replacement number two. Here, come and sit down and warm yourself up. Would you like a cup of tea?"

"No thanks. One thing they're not short of at local group meetings is tea."

"I suppose not. How's that charming husband of yours?"

"Looking forward to the Christmas holidays. Well, the bits of it that are left when he's back from taking Year Ten skiing."

"And Ellie?"

Barbara rolls her eyes. "You don't want to know. I'm sure I was never that obnoxious as a teenager. Was I?"

"You had your moments, if I remember your mother's

letters rightly. But it was a question of absence making the heart grow fonder. You were always perfectly delightful when I saw you on my home visits. You used to ask politely about life in the tropics as though you were really interested."

"But I was! Just as Daniel used to be – still is, of course."

"He's a love. I can't imagine many other young men bothering to write to their ancient great-aunt. I keep threatening to visit him, you know."

"He told me. He'd love it if you did."

"Well, who knows. I may go next winter if I'm still alive."

"I'm sure you will be."

"This growing old business. It really has nothing whatsoever to recommend it."

"What about wisdom?"

"What about wisdom?" says Eleanor Cameron wryly.

Barbara Maddison holds her hands out to the fire. There is something about her aunt's tone of voice, a weariness that she has not noticed before. Perhaps there is something they could do to bring her hip operation forward. Then she notices a large cardboard box beside the fireplace. Aunt Eleanor's eyes follow hers.

"I thought it was high time I cleared out the attic."

"You never got that box down by yourself?"

"Now don't start telling me I'm too old to do that kind of thing, Barbara, dear. If you hadn't dropped in, you'd never have known about it."

"And you could be lying at the bottom of the attic ladder, crushed by a ton of memorabilia."

"Well, I'm not, as you can see. And some of it is very interesting. You know, I found my original ticket – for my first voyage out. It brought back such strong memories – tastes, smells, sights, the lot."

"What else is in there?"

"Letters, diaries, photographs – that kind of thing. Hence the roaring fire."

"You're not burning them?"

"I've made a start."

"Aunt Eleanor!"

"What?"

"How could you destroy all that wonderful stuff?"

"If I didn't, you'd have to. I may as well save you the trouble."

"But it's your past."

"Exactly – my past."

"May I have a look?"

Barbara kneels down beside the box. It is still half full. She picks out a carved wooden box and holds it out to her aunt.

"This is lovely."

Eleanor Cameron takes it from her and opens it. She pulls out a handful of photographs. "You can have the box if you like. The Emir of Kano gave it to me."

"Are you sure? Thank you."

Eleanor puts on her glasses and flicks through the photographs quickly, then pauses to look at one of them more closely. A young woman in a loose flowery dress is sitting on a cane chair on an open veranda. In front of her are three glasses and a decanter on a cane table. To her left, his hand resting on her shoulder, is a tall man with dark curly hair. Another man, sporting a moustache, is sitting to her right, grinning out at the camera. There is a pot of bougainvillaea on the corner of each step. Purple, they'd been bright purple, she remembers.

"Who are they?" asks Barbara, crouching beside Eleanor's chair.

"That's me."

"It isn't!"

"I haven't always been eighty-one, you know."

"I didn't mean that – I just don't think I've seen pictures of you in Nigeria."

"That's because I didn't keep any. Or thought I didn't."

"Why not?"

"Oh, you know …"

"Who's the man standing next to you?"

Eleanor Cameron does not reply for a while. A log crackles and spits in the hearth. A sudden gust of wind rattles the sash windows.

"Thomas Kayne," she says at last. "He was a lawyer in the Colonial Service. We shared an office at one time."

There is something about the way she says it that suggests no more information about him will be forthcoming. Barbara knows her aunt better than to probe.

"And the very handsome chap sitting there?"

"Stanley Shea. He was a surveyor. They were close friends. Him and Thomas Kayne. We all were. I'm trying to think who took the photograph. Musa Mohammed! It must've been him – Stanley Shea's house-boy. He loved any kind of gadget. He was such a bright lad. Wasted as a servant. He married shortly after this photograph was taken. A lovely girl – Jamila, she was called. I paid for their children's education. And their grandchildren's for that matter."

"That was good of you – to sponsor them through school."

"Not really. Sometimes I think that was probably the most useful thing I did in all my years in West Africa."

"Oh, Aunt Eleanor! You can't really think that!"

"Why ever not?" She looks at the picture again, then tosses it into the fire. It blackens, curls and is gone, leaving nothing but a grey wisp.

Barbara looks at her aunt. She is staring into the flames, her expression unreadable.

"May I see the rest of them?"

"If you like."

Eleanor passes her the pictures, her hand trembling slightly. Barbara Maddison looks at the photographs. There are some of landscapes and settlements, festivals and formal ceremonies, but most are of people, and most are of the two men in the first photograph.

"Are you still in touch with any of them – apart from Musa Mohammed?"

"He died many years ago. But his grandson still writes – and with rather fewer grammatical errors than some Oxford graduates I could name."

"And the others?" asks Barbara, trying to sound non-specific.

"I lost touch with them years ago."

"Weren't you curious to find out what happened to them?"

"I know what happened to them. One of them disappeared and the other was badly injured in a shooting accident and ended up in a nursing home on the South Coast. He's probably long dead. The Sandersons used to visit him – James Sanderson had been the District Governor – but I've not heard from them for a few years now. And I think that's quite enough reminiscing for one day, don't you?"

Eleanor Cameron takes the photographs from her niece, and holds them towards the fire. Then she appears to change her mind and puts them back into the cardboard box.

"Now, Barbara, I don't know about you, but I could do with a drink – and I don't mean tea."

Daniel stood at the top of the cliff and looked out over the sea. On the horizon two wooden fishing boats, their sails billowing in the cool evening breeze, were silhouetted against a pink, purple and orange sky. He felt as though he was merging into a postcard of the type he enjoyed sending his cousin Lucy, who shared his love of high kitsch. As he walked down the cliff path he could make out a small thatched hut, with low wooden benches and tables precariously arranged on the sand in front of it. Two large, colourful shapes were sitting side by side on the bench furthest from the bar. By the time he reached the beach, the sky had turned a uniform greyish mauve.

"I took you two at your word. I hope you don't mind."

Isabel looked up from her novel, and smiled broadly. "Daniel! How lovely. Paddy, be an angel and get the boy a drink."

Patrick doffed his canvas hat and shuffled to the bar.

Isabel put her hand on Daniel's arm. "How are you, my dear? We were wondering if you'd join us sometime. You see, we are as predictable as you probably feared we were. We love this place. Bakari has taken to sending up one of his children to see if we are OK if we ever miss our sundowner. Did you see that wonderful sunset? Each time I think it can't get any better, the next one is even more fantastic."

"Is the old girl boasting about that stud of a husband who pleasures her senseless? Still, you can't blame her," said Patrick, placing three bottles of beer on the table, and thrusting his hips into Isabel's face as he did so.

"Just ignore him, Daniel. Laughing only encourages him."

"What have you got in there?" asked Patrick, nodding at the parcel on the bench beside Daniel. "A stash of confiscated cannabis? The ultimate High Commission perk?"

"Nothing so exciting, unless you get a high out of fuchsia-patterned pink damask."

"I'll try anything once. Bring any of those jumbo-size Rizlas, Izzy?"

Isabel gave Patrick an affectionately withering look. "You see, Daniel. You shouldn't encourage him. Who's it for?"

"And you say I'm always prying into other people's business," Patrick interrupted.

"It's for … Well, I don't know, really." As he said it, Daniel realised how ridiculous he must sound. "I just bought it."

"Do you make a habit of spontaneous cloth purchasing?" asked Patrick with genuine interest.

"No. I don't. It was all a bit of an accident really." Daniel fiddled with the knots on the parcel. He could see her long fingers weaving the string backwards and forwards, then tensing as she tied the knots.

"Let's see it. I love material. May I?" Isabel took the parcel from Daniel and tore open a corner. "That's gorgeous."

"You can have it, if you like it."

"No, I couldn't possibly. Keep it. There's bound to be a wedding or a naming ceremony or something. It'll make a wonderful present for somebody. Didn't you say that your gardener friend had two wives? I'm sure they'd look lovely in it. I haven't seen this pattern before – it must have just come in. Where did you get it?"

"I'll leave you two ladies to your girls' talk. Give me a shout when it's all over and I'll come back for that beer our new friend owes me." Patrick got up and walked to the edge of the sand. He rolled up his trousers and waded calf-deep along the beach, pausing every few yards to greet the beach vendors and bargain for fruit which he placed carefully in his hat.

"Sorry about him," Isabel said, nodding in the direction of her husband.

Daniel put the parcel back on the bench beside him. "It's from one of those Lebanese shops."

"Not the one on Canal Street? Where that …"

"Yes. She seemed fine. I mean, she appeared to have got home safely."

"Well that's a relief. Though it didn't look as though that was the first time she had done that."

"Still, I wish I had done something to help."

"Daniel, tell me it's none of my business, but are you having some kind of relationship with this woman?"

"No!"

"But you'd like to be?"

"Like to be what?"

"Having a relationship with her?" Isabel wondered why he seemed so agitated. She wanted to hug him.

"No. It's nothing like that. I hadn't spoken to her until today."

"Listen. Despite what my dear husband implies, going into a shop that sells cloth isn't a crime against humanity. And I don't think that having an interest in thin blonde women is a punishable offence either. You don't have to say anything about it if you don't want to, my dear."

"She's called Rachel. I've just found that out. I don't know anything else about her. Not really."

"What makes her so interesting? Is she very beautiful? I didn't really notice yesterday."

"No. Well, yes. But that's not it. There's something about her that ... that's just so incongruous."

Isabel looked at him expectantly but did not interrupt.

"I first noticed her the week I arrived – months ago – buying fruit at the market," continued Daniel. "She was having a furious argument, in what sounded like fluent Bakawa, with a man who had tried to sell her bad oranges. She let rip at him. Like some avenging pre-Raphaelite."

"Rather more Giacometti than Rossetti, I'd say."

"After that, I saw her around the city once or twice. Always alone, always walking as though there was no one else in the whole place – just separate from everything. She definitely wasn't a tourist, and she didn't seem like a volunteer or aid worker or anyone like that. I just couldn't think what she could be doing here. Then I saw her working in that cloth shop in Canal Street and it made even less sense."

"Why?"

"You'd understand if you saw her there. She looks so bizarrely out of place. Always dressed in black. Always reading. Selling something she clearly has no interest in for someone she barely speaks to. I can't stop wondering what she's doing here. How she came to be living such a strange life."

"Aren't we all?"

"All what?"

"Living strange lives in strange places – away from our so-called natural habitats?"

"But she seems so … so … sad."

"How on earth would you know that from a couple of sightings through a shop window?"

"I went in today."

"Hence the material?"

"Yes. Look, Isabel. There is something else. But you'll think I'm completely mad."

"Go on."

"I think I know her."

"But you just said you didn't know anything about her."

"When I first saw her face in the market, I thought – for a second or two – that I recognised her. But then when she spoke to the trader in Bakawa I knew it couldn't be her."

"Couldn't be who?"

"Rachel Kayne. But every time I saw her, I felt less sure that it wasn't her. And every time I thought about it later, I felt more sure that it couldn't be her. If you see what I mean. Well, I did say you'd think I was mad. And today. When I found out she was called Rachel. It was just such a weird coincidence. Am I making any sense at all?"

"Not really. But carry on. I'm fascinated. Tell me more about this Rachel Kayne who probably isn't her at all."

"When I was at Oxford, I used to sing in the college choir. There was this amazing singer who'd be brought in for special concerts. She was studying something like Oriental Studies, I think. She had one of those voices that made you feel your heart was literally soaring. She was – I don't know – incredibly vivacious. She had a wonderful laugh. We nicknamed her Zuleika. She wore the most amazing clothes. The rest of us would be wandering about in jeans and sweatshirts and there she'd be dressed in the most beautiful scarves and leather boots and silk skirts."

"But what was she really like?"

"I never really knew her. She was just one of those people that everyone recognised and everyone knew something about. I don't think she was ever involved with anyone in particular but you never saw her alone. She hung out with the other beautiful people – the acting crowd, mostly – they seemed to gravitate towards her."

"I have to say, Daniel, that it seems unlikely, from this description at least, that she's the same woman as our Rachel in the cloth shop ..."

" ... who wears black, never smiles, is always alone, and is a fluent Bakawa speaker. I know. I thought that's what you'd think."

"The hunter-gatherer has returned and will be expecting a lot of fornication in return for these fruits of the forest." Patrick emptied a hatful of bananas and mangoes onto Isabel's lap and kissed her on the lips. He bent down to unroll his trousers over his damp white calves.

"You'll get a lot of squashed banana on your head if you put that filthy thing on again," Isabel observed.

Patrick looked into his hat and grimaced. "I trust the conversation has moved on from haberdashery?"

"We were talking about misfits actually – not that you would know anything about that, Paddy."

Patrick turned his empty beer bottle upside down and made exaggerated shaking gestures. Daniel walked over to the bar and returned with two bottles.

"Aren't you having another?" Patrick asked.

"I think I'll go home. It's been a long and rather odd day. But I'll come again, if that's OK."

"We'd be offended if you didn't, wouldn't we, Izzy?"

Isabel stood up and hugged Daniel tightly, then gave him a kiss on the forehead. "We certainly would. And, Daniel – there's one way you could find out if you're right."

"How?"

"You could always ask her."

Daniel smiled, picked up his parcel, then turned and headed up the cliff path.

"What a sweet boy," said Isabel, watching him as he disappeared round a bend in the path.

"Another one for your collection?" Patrick asked affectionately as he wiped the condensation from the bottle. "Cheers, you old fag hag."

"Wonderful kibbeh, Rachel, you must tell me how you make it." Suhad put down her knife and fork and dabbed her lips with a napkin. Bright red lipstick smiled up from the starched white of the cloth. "And the couscous was cooked to perfection."

"If you're not careful, you'll turn into quite an accomplished Lebanese wife, eh, Rachel?" Faysal laughed as he lit one of the strong French cigarettes that he imported.

Suhad wove her delicate gold and platinum necklace between her finely manicured fingers.

"I had the most wonderful *loubia bi zeit* the other day, Rachel. Lamya brought the green beans back from her holiday in Egypt and the cook prepared them beautifully."

Faysal pushed his chair back and blew a perfect smoke ring, then another which floated through it as it hovered above his head. He turned to Kamal. "Business good?"

"Not bad. Rachel is managing things in Canal Street. I'm hardly there these days. The warehouses on McCarthy Street should be finished next month. Ready for the new deliveries."

"You're still importing from Holland?"

"Yes, but China is where it's at now. I'll be there buying for a couple of months in the New Year."

"Any plans for the Eid holiday, Rachel?" asked Suhad.

"No. I'll be staying in the house." Rachel pushed her plate away from her, the kibbeh, couscous and salad barely touched.

"Rachel objects to the mass slaughter of innocent goats, don't you, darling?" said Kamal.

"We're going to Dakar," said Suhad, looking at Rachel's plate. "Why don't you both come too?"

"I'll be in China then. But Rachel will go."

"No. Thank you. I'd prefer to stay here."

"But darling," said Suhad, "we'd have a wonderful time. Think of the shopping."

"I think I spend enough time in shops. But thank you for asking."

A vein in Kamal's forehead began to pulsate.

"What about that swimming pool idea?" said Faysal. "Still going to go ahead with it?"

"Yes, though we'll lose a lot of the garden. There's been a bit of opposition," said Kamal, nodding towards Rachel. "But it'll be started before the rains."

"Are you all right?" Suhad asked Rachel. "You look rather pale."

Rachel, who had been staring out into the garden, stood up. "I think I'll go to bed. Sorry. I'll ask the maid to serve coffee on the veranda." She caught Kamal's gaze and held it for a few seconds, defying him to stop her leaving.

"It was lovely to see you." Suhad got up and kissed the air by Rachel's cheeks with her deep red lips. "I hope you feel better soon. Ring me if you change your mind about Senegal."

"Thank you. I'm sure I will. Feel better. Goodnight. Goodnight, Faysal. Please, don't get up."

In her room, Rachel lay on the bed, her hands behind her head, staring up at the high wooden ceiling and listening to the low voices coming from the veranda. She could smell strong black coffee, cardamom, and cigarette smoke. She heard her name and held her breath, trying to catch what Kamal was saying. "Very tired, with all …" Another voice, Suhad's now. "Must be such a disappointment … I'm sure it'll happen … It took us much longer than we thought it would …" Then Faysal. "So all the frangipanis will have to go?" The murmur of voices became quieter. She turned over and shut her eyes.

She is swimming in a pool of thick, sticky blood, trying to push her hair out of her face. Kamal is leaning over the pool. He is telling Faysal that swimming pools are not as expensive as you'd think they would be. Suhad is standing at the side of the pool. "Daniel Maddison, Aid Attaché," she sings as she tears a gold-embossed card into tiny pieces and lets them drop, one by one, into the water. Rachel raises a hand to Kamal. He reaches down into the red depths but does not take it. He pulls up a baby. It is still attached to Rachel by a cord of pink fuchsia-patterned damask. Kamal yanks the baby towards him with one hand and pushes her under the bloody water with the other. "Tahir! Come back," she screams as her lungs fill with blood. "For Christ's sake, come back."

Rachel woke with a start. She could see Kamal watching her in the darkness as he unbuttoned his shirt. The light from the security lamps outside caught the thick black hairs on his chest and forearms.

"What time is it?" she asked.

Kamal looked at his watch as he took it off. "Nearly two."

He undressed slowly, looking at her all the time as he

did so. She could see that he was already erect.

"A very pleasant evening. Just a shame you weren't there to enjoy it too. Do you always have to do that?"

"Do what?"

"Go to bed in the middle of dinner. Say you're sick. I don't like it. People will think I am married to an invalid."

"We're not married."

"I think you know what I mean, Rachel."

"No, not really. And I didn't say I was ill. Suhad did."

"You hardly said a word the whole evening."

"I didn't have anything to say."

"Well, there are other ways to communicate. As you know, my darling." Kamal's voice was cold and urgent.

She turned her face away as he knelt on the bed between her legs. He reached forward and began to unbutton her nightdress. She felt the hairs on his knuckles brushing against her bare skin. Grasping her shoulders, he pushed her thighs apart with his knees and sank down into her. She shut her eyes.

As he rolled off, she could feel his semen trickling down the inside of her thighs. He lay very still for a few moments, then got up without touching her and felt his way across the room and through the carved wooden door that separated her room from his. She heard the fan in his room begin to turn and the sounds of the bed creaking as he climbed into it.

Rachel lay in the dark, listening to the quiet tick of his watch on the table beside her. After a while, she did up her buttons, got up and walked out of her room and onto the veranda. Her nightdress clung to her damp thighs. She stepped down into the garden, feeling the warm stone of the path under her feet, and breathing in the scent of the frangipani trees. She fingered the silky yellow petals and smooth branches. She heard the chink of the watchdog's chain as he lifted his head, then the dull thud of his tail wagging against the wooden wall of his kennel. She could see the outline of the watchman, squatting outside the locked gates, wrapped in a blanket, and the glow of the charcoal in his small tin burner. She heard him cough, then spit loudly.

Rachel wrapped her arms around herself and looked up at the sky. Some nights she saw shooting stars but tonight the stars were still. She willed one to stop its ridiculous cheery twinkling and plunge down into oblivion. She wiped her tears away angrily but they continued to flow.

He is lying in his nightshirt under the mahogany desk, lining up small ebony carvings of animals that someone must have given to his father. It is late. His mother thinks he is in bed but he loves to hide in the library and watch her as she works. A fire is burning in the grate. His father is at a big dinner at the Chamber of Commerce. Something to do with the Governor of Nigeria, he had said as he left. Nigeria. Where is that, he wonders. Is it across the Mersey? And why does it need governing anyway? Stanley hears the front door open, hears his father saying something to the maid. The library door opens. Stanley moves the elephant to the front of the line.

"You will never guess, Madeleine, what that scoundrel Lord Leverhulme said." His father's voice is clear and angry. He does not wait for a reply. Stanley stops playing and listens.

"He said that – and I quote – 'the West African races have to be treated very much as one would treat children when they are immature and underdeveloped'. Leverhulme and all his cronies should be horse-whipped. And that's not all. He claims – and I'm quite serious, Madeleine – that 'the African native will be happier when his labour is directed by his white brother'. Leverhulme may as well be advocating a return to slavery."

"What's the African native?" says Stanley from under the table.

He hears his mother get up and walk towards the table. He sees her shoes, and a hand reaching down towards him. He knows he has lost his hiding place for ever.

"Up you ..."

" … get, Stan. There's someone to see you. We can't be having you lying there with soup stains all over you, can we now?"

Vera delves into the bedside locker and rummages around for a clean pyjama jacket. Stanley Shea feels strong arms grip his shoulders and lever him out of his high metal bed and into a chair. He feels hands undoing his buttons, catching the thin white hairs of his concave chest. He feels cold plastic against his back. He sees a shadow pass his face as someone or something moves in front of him.

"There you are, my love. That's much better." Vera combs Stanley's wispy hair with her fingers. "You look quite respectable now. Here, come in, dear." She gestures to a beige plastic chair. An elderly woman, who has been waiting in the doorway, walks in and sits down stiffly.

"I'll get you a nice cup of tea, Miss Cameron." Vera gathers up the dirty linen in both arms and pushes the door open with her ample rump.

"Hello, Stanley," says Eleanor Cameron. She takes one of Stanley's hands and holds it in both of hers. "It's been a long time." She stops, keeping her eyes on their entwined fingers, wondering what to say, where to begin. She forces herself to look at Stanley Shea's face. There are cavities where there should be flesh, and a deep wound in place of an eye. The scars, long healed, follow a gnarled course across one side of his face. His remaining eye, a milky, rheumy blue, stares ahead, blinking from time to time. Eleanor Cameron looks away. She had seen many more terrible things during her forty years in West Africa. She was in Biafra during the war, after all. But sitting here, in this drearily chintzy nursing home, remembering Stanley Shea as the eccentric, brilliant man he had been, she feels something akin to grief.

"Here you are, my love," says Vera, putting an institution-blue china cup and saucer on the bedside locker.

"Thank you," says Eleanor Cameron quietly. "How much can he see?"

"We don't know for sure. He seems to know when people come in. We think he can hear but of course he can't speak, poor dear. Well, when I say can't, it's more like won't – the naughty boy!"

Eleanor Cameron winces. She wants to gather Stanley up and take him far away from this cheerless place. But where would they go? They are both of them strangers in their own country now, living out cold, arthritic retirements, victims of their strong constitutions.

"Did you know him out there? Africa wasn't it?" asks Vera as she re-makes the bed.

"Yes. For many years. There was a group of us – friends – in the Colonial Service."

"That must have been nice," says Vera.

"Yes. It was ... it was." Eleanor Cameron suddenly feels too weary to engage in even the most superficial of conversations. She squeezes Stanley's hand, willing him to squeeze back, but the hand remains limp in hers.

"I'll come back tomorrow," she says to Vera. "I've been travelling all day and I'm not feeling quite myself. I'm staying with some friends who retired to Worthing. Is there a particularly good time to visit?"

"One hour is much the same as another, I think." Vera gives the sheets a final pat. "Perhaps after breakfast. He seems happier when it's light."

Eleanor Cameron gets up and walks towards the door. Vera rearranges Stanley in his chair, then gives his locker a cursory wipe with a grimy, damp cloth.

"There you go, my dear. That's better," she says and follows Miss Cameron out of the room.

Stanley Shea's hand now feels an emptiness where, only moments ago, there had been warmth. His head slumps forward. His one eye closes. He breathes in the smell of mildew and disinfectant.

He is at the quayside in Liverpool with his father. Tall dockers stare at them and spit as they walk by the vast warehouses towards the ship. Stanley sees that it is called the SS Investigator. *He thinks this is odd, as it is his father who is supposed to be doing the investigating. They walk up the gangplank. His father speaks to the captain who has a face of stone, set in a sneer. They are led towards a small cabin in the heart of the ship. Stanley smells seaweed and mildew. The captain knocks on the door. It is opened by a young whey-faced sailor.*

Standing in the middle of the cabin, his hands tied behind his back, naked from the waist up, is a man with skin so black it looks almost blue. Stanley stares. He cannot take his eyes off the black man. Hair as tightly curled as sheep's wool. Strange symmetrical scars, like cats' whiskers, on the sides of his face. Stanley wonders if the man's eyes, which are staring at the floor, are blue like his own or black like the man's skin. He sees his father touch the man's arm. The man looks up. Huge dark brown eyes. Stanley feels tears well up. He wants to weep for pity, for the sheer beauty of the black-skinned man.

Vera passes Stanley's room again on her way to her tea break. She puts her head round the door. "That bad eye giving you trouble again, Stan?" she says, wiping away the tears from his face with a corner of her apron. "Never mind. There's worse things happen at sea."

The deck of the ferry seethed with women on their way to market. Daniel found himself wedged between a couple of market traders. He tried to focus on the extraordinary grace of the dolphins which leapt in the wake of the ferry, rather than the fact that there was only one visible life jacket and several hundred non-swimmers on board. Daniel mused over the moral dilemma. Would he swim to shore as fast as he could, away from the scores of clutching, flailing arms, or attempt, nobly but hopelessly, to save a few of the women before being dragged down into the depths of the river? It was always a difficult one.

It had been a ghastly day. For reasons that were no longer very clear to him, he had been asked to accompany the EC horticulture adviser to the North Bank to look at a women's gardening project. Mr Smets was a powerfully built, middle-aged Belgian. He had a moustache that Daniel could only think of as Hitleresque, small, dark, weasly eyes, and an abundance of black hair that he slicked back with the Belgian equivalent of Brylcreem.

On their arrival at the communal garden, a group of women had presented them with a gift of tomatoes and okra on dishes of banana leaves and then performed a short dance. Mr Smets stood up. Daniel had assumed he was going to make a speech thanking them for the gifts and the entertainment. To his horror, the horticulture adviser had issued a string of quite extraordinary invective. Why were the women spending so much time on their own gardens? Why were there weeds between the rows of vegetables? Why were they dancing and drumming when they should be working? Why were the yields so much lower than he had predicted? People with their attitude to work were not worth spending any money on. The interpreter had faltered as he translated Mr Smets's heavily accented English. Daniel hoped that he was adapting the tirade rather liberally, but could not tell. The women had looked slightly surprised but still managed to smile as the shrill words rang across the garden. In a life which had had its share of excruciatingly embarrassing moments, quite a few of them since his arrival in Bakinabe, Daniel could think of none to rival this one.

As the ferry neared the shore, he could make out the city mosque, the riverside warehouses, the prison and a couple of cafés. The café owners had made valiant attempts, with their jaunty parasols and waterside tables, to create a Riviera ambience. They had very nearly succeeded, foiled only by the stench of decaying fish, the grimy froth that lapped at the shore, and the odd human turd that bobbed in on the tide. Daniel had soon learnt to order the strongest Lebanese coffee and to look out at the horizon rather than down at the beach. The ferry docked with a lurch and crunch and the passengers streamed off towards the market. He offered up silent thanks for safe delivery and walked along the bank to his favourite café, furthest from the ferry.

Ibraima, the proprietor, was standing looking out at the street. He had spent many years as a cook on British merchant ships, and his English was extremely good. Though he rarely ventured out of his café, he had an uncanny knack of knowing about everything that was going on in the city. He smiled broadly as Daniel took his hand and shook it warmly.

"*Salaamalekum*, Ibraima."

"*Malekumsalaam*, Mr Daniel. Long time. Where have you been? How are you and how is work?"

"Don't even ask."

"Don't ask? Why? Have you transferred to MI5?"

"No, no. Nothing like that. This place is looking great. New umbrellas, I see. And new posters."

"The brewery delivered them today. *Lion Brew beer. Won't cost you dear. You'll have good cheer. For three lamasi clear.* Very catchy, don't you think?"

"Very. How's work with you, anyway?"

"Work's fine. And how is your family?"

"They're fine, as far as I know," said Daniel, remembering as he said it that his mother owed him a letter.

"That's good. That's very good. What can I get you? A Lion Brew?"

"No thanks. A Lebanese coffee please. Not too much sugar."

Ibraima went into the kitchen leaving Daniel to gaze at the faint outline of the opposite riverbank. He wondered about alternative careers. Perhaps he should become an advertising copywriter: *Mr Smets. He is the pits. An also-ran. Our EC man.*

Ibraima put a small cup and saucer on the table and poured out the thick black coffee. "How is that brother of mine?" he asked. "Working hard, I hope."

Daniel did not know if Baboucar was a brother in the sense of "same mother same father" but was aware that he was some kind of relative of Ibraima's. "He's very well indeed. Binta Two is expecting again."

"Another son, I hope."

"Well, daughters are lovely too, don't you think?"

"Sure, but lovely is not enough. Just think of the dowries they will be needing."

"That's a long time off. By then, with this place, you'll be a millionaire and will be able to provide your nieces with all the cloth and jewels they could wish for."

Ibraima laughed loudly and slapped him on the back. "I hope so, Mr Daniel, I hope so."

"Speaking of cloth," said Daniel, stirring up the sludge at the bottom of his cup, watching it swirl and settle again. "Do you know anything about the cloth merchants on Canal Street?"

"Cloth merchants?"

"Yes, you know, the wholesalers. There are lots of them."

"What is it you want to know? My wife is the one to ask where to buy the best cloth."

"Do you know that very big one, on the corner by the canal?"

"H. A. Sharif and Sons? Of course. Who doesn't? The family used to own most of the warehouses here. And much else besides. They are still the biggest importers in the country."

"What's he like, this H. A. Sharif?"

"A pile of bones, I should think." Ibraima laughed. "He died about forty years ago. It's run by one of his grandsons – Kamal Sharif."

"Is he the only one who works in the business?"

"The cloth business, yes. Another brother – Faysal – trades in tobacco and vehicles. There's one who lives in the States. Some kind of doctor, I think. Then there was one who died four or five years ago. And I think there's a couple of sisters too."

"So what's Kamal Sharif like?"

"Kamal? Rich. Very rich. He has a reputation as a – what's the word you have – a fixer."

"Is he married?"

"No, I don't think so, but he has a—"

"Blimey, if it isn't Damian. How are you, mate? You dicing with death too, eating in a local hostelry?" Bob Newpin pulled up a chair and sat down heavily, wiping his forehead with a small damp towel that hung round his neck.

"It's Daniel."

"Yeah, whatever. HERE, BOY, GET US A DRINK. A beer, Damian?"

"No thanks. I was just going."

"Oh, go on. TWO BEERS, BOY." Newpin spoke loudly and slowly. "AND MAKE SURE THEY'RE COLD." Ibraima gave Daniel a sympathetic look and took a couple of bottles of Lion Brew out of the fridge.

"Very friendly, the locals, I find. Not much up top, though." Newpin spread his legs widely and tipped back on the chair. "Not a bad little gaff here. Bit of a pong though. Do you come here often, so to speak? Ah, that's the ticket. PUT THEM DOWN HERE. COMPRENDO?"

"I trust that the beverage will be to your satisfaction and hope, most sincerely, that you will have an enjoyable stay in our country," said Ibraima, winking at Daniel as he turned away. Daniel heard a roar of laughter coming from the kitchen.

"Well, fuck a duck!" Newpin appeared temporarily

lost for words. Then he drained the bottle in a few loud gulps. "You going back to HQ? I wouldn't say no to a lift if you twisted my arm."

"My car's by the ferry office."

"Brilliant. How much is a couple of beers, then? I can't get to grips with this bloody Monopoly money."

"Ninety lamasi."

"What, each?"

"Yes. And a ten per cent tip is customary."

"Sounds fair enough." Newpin took out some sticky banknotes and put them on the table. "Off we go then, Damian. No peace for the wicked, eh?"

Brighton, February 25th 1992

POST CARD

THE ADDRESS TO BE WRITTEN ON THIS SIDE

I thought of you yesterday
evening at the premier of
Jonathon Rosen's Oratorio.
You would have loved it.
Jonathon was there - taking
a bow - looking tanned and
happy. He has clearly moved
on. I hope you have too.
You deserve happiness -
it's an emotion I've grown to
appreciate. R x

Daniel Maddison
FCO Tiakunda
c/o King Charles St.
London SW1A 2AH

Patrick Redmond sat at his desk sucking the end of a small, blunt pencil. Every so often, he scribbled down a couple of words, looked at them for a few moments, then irritably crossed them out again. He sighed, deeply and theatrically, and looked out of the window. His eyes lit up as he saw Isabel struggling through the front gate. He watched her heave her shopping bags up the steps of the veranda, then walked out to meet her.

"At last. I thought you'd never come home. I haven't written a thing since you left. I need some inspiration."

"I've heard from a very reputable source that unloading the shopping can be a tremendous source of literary stimulation."

"I can think of a much more interesting form of stimulation than that."

"So can I, but the yoghurt will curdle, the milk will go off and we'll miss Mass again."

"A small price to pay for being transported to Paradise."

Isabel kissed him. "Flattery will get you nowhere – at least for the next three hours. After that, this could be your lucky day."

"What's that?" asked Patrick, looking at the small package that Isabel had just taken out of one of the bags. "Don't tell me that the accidental buying of garish cloth is catching? We must get you vaccinated before the house is swamped with little bags oozing puce polyester."

"What are you talking about? And I bet you don't even know what colour puce is. Here, put the milk in the fridge, my love."

"It's a slippery slope."

"To where? And can you put these oranges in a bowl?"

"Which bowl?"

"Any bowl you like."

"Really, Isabel, genius like mine shouldn't be wasted on domestic trivia."

"Patrick Redmond! It's domestic trivia that keeps you fed and clothed and—"

"Only joking, my darling. You know I love it when you give me that look. It makes my skin tingle."

Isabel took the bag of oranges out of Patrick's hands and tipped them into the bowl on the table.

"Mariama was in town," she said. "She's looking so much happier now she's not working for Fenella Moss. She asked when you next wanted her. I said tomorrow afternoon. Was that right?"

"Yes, the light's best then. How was she?"

"Busy selling batik skirts to pasty tourists."

"I don't suppose that's all she was selling them, silly girl."

"Patrick, I really don't think that you should feel responsible for the moral well-being of half the city's nubile under-eighteens. If that's the way Mariama wants to earn her living – and we don't even know if that is what she's doing – it's up to her, isn't it? Is there really so much difference between prostitution and posing naked for your blessed photographs?"

"Of course there is. That's art. The other is … well, not art anyway. Have you read the latest HIV statistics? They're terrifying."

"I'm sure she's careful. She jolly well ought to be, after all the chats I've had with her and all the money I've spent buying her condoms. Goodness knows what the man in the shop thought when a plump old *toubab* came in to buy fifty Durex."

"Probably thought you would make someone a very happy man. And he'd be right." Patrick hugged Isabel tightly. "Tell me, my love," he whispered in her ear. "What have you got in that parcel?"

"You brute!" Isabel laughed. "I thought you were going to say something deeply romantic then." She tore open the package and spread out the cloth on the table.

"My God! Pope John Paul II! It's absolutely fantastic. Where on earth did you get it?"

"That huge wholesalers on Canal Street. I couldn't resist it. I thought I'd get a shirt made up for Joe. Next time he and Lucy go to a bad taste party, he'll be the beau of the ball."

"Is there enough for two? I bet Father Seamus would die for a Pope John Paul II shirt."

"I think so. I'll ask Mariama's mother to make them up for me. I saw her, you know," she said, as she folded up the material and put it on the chair by the door.

"Saw who? Mariama's mother?"

"No. That woman who had the argument in the road, the one that Daniel told me about."

"Where?"

"In the shop. I bought that material from her. I don't think she recognised me."

"What was she like?"

"Just as Daniel described her. Very thin, very fair and very silent."

"Sounds a bundle of laughs. We must have her to dinner."

"I can see why he finds her fascinating."

"Why?"

"What was the word he used? Incongruous, that was it."

"Isn't that the pot calling the kettle black, or whatever the cliché is?"

"What do you mean?" asked Isabel.

"Well, Daniel's hardly the typical foreign office type, is he? He must make old Alec very jittery. The combination of intelligence and integrity must be highly threatening to someone who has the intellect of a pudding and the social conscience of an anopheles mosquito. Not to mention Daniel's pretty face, with those lovely cheekbones and big dark blue eyes. Your words, not mine, I hasten to add. Chinless wonders from Cheam are more usual in his position, don't you think?"

"In our experience. But maybe we've just been unlucky."

"One decent High Commission official in over thirty-five years can't just be bad luck."

"Who knows? Anyway, she was very polite."

"Who?"

"The woman in the shop. Rachel."

"Why shouldn't she have been?"

"No reason. I just wasn't sure what to expect. I think I know what Daniel was trying to say. There was something pretty bleak about her."

"Perhaps we really should invite her for dinner. Cheer her up. I could tell her my joke about the Englishman, the Irishman and the Lebanese."

"That would probably tip her over the edge."

"Is she on the edge?" Patrick looked concerned.

"No. I mean I couldn't possibly say from a five-minute encounter in a shop, but not happy, I'd say."

"Well, nor am I. I haven't written a decent poem in weeks."

"It'll come. It always does."

"Maybe I'll never write another one."

"You always say that, and then you produce something marvellous."

"Come to bed, Izzy, my muse. Soothe my fevered brow."

"I know that euphemism, Paddy. You'll have to think of something better than that."

Patrick sat down at the desk again while Isabel tidied the last of the groceries away. She looked up from the cupboard and saw him sitting with his eyes shut. As she walked out onto the veranda and sat down to open the post, she heard the familiar scratching as he started to write.

Daniel sat in his office joining up paper clips. When he had used up all the clips, he held up the chain and gazed at it as it dangled to the floor. It was about the most productive thing he had done all day and by far the most enjoyable. He looked at the pile of files on his desk and decided it was time for a break. As he walked out of the door, he collided with the High Commissioner's secretary.

"Danny boy! Where are you going, you naughty thing? Off on some secret assignation, don't tell me. No, don't. Really. You'll break my heart, you wicked boy."

Sandra Didsbury had large, glossy-red lips, and what Daniel supposed could be described as seriously big hair. She was wearing a very short, tight, floral skirt and a bright red satin blouse that gaped between each straining button, on which she had pinned a flashing Father Christmas brooch. Her thick little legs ended abruptly in a pair of shiny black pumps. As usual, Daniel found himself trying to work out who it was she reminded him of. As usual, the answer eluded him.

"There's a letter here for you somewhere, I think. Yes, here it is," she said, pulling out an airmail envelope from the pile of post she was carrying. "Definitely a woman's writing. Anyone we ought to know about? Any serious rival for my affections?"

Daniel took the envelope from her. "No, you're in luck. It's from my mother."

"Oh, that's what they all say. You can't fool me."

"I'm afraid it really is. By the way, Sandra, has that Bob Newpin been in again?"

"Why, are you jealous? You needn't be. I go for the strong, dark, silent types myself."

"I just wondered what he's up to. I keep bumping into him in the most unlikely places."

"I think he's been having discussions with Len in Commercial. I don't know what about. I could find out, though." Sandra puckered up her lips and shut her eyes. "For a small fee."

"You'd get a terrible shock if I did kiss you one day."

"Just try me, lover boy."

"And be had up for bribery and corruption?"

"You can corrupt me any day, sweetheart. Just a shame you're thirty years too late."

Sandra shrieked with laughter. Daniel smiled as she shimmied fatly down the corridor. As he went back into his office, he realised, with some despondency, that he preferred Sandra's amiable sexual harassment to the company of any of the rest of the expatriate High Commission staff.

Len Barling, the Commercial Attaché, was in a league of his own in the ghastly stakes. It was a mystery to Daniel why Len should have chosen a career in which overseas travel would inevitably feature, given that he had a deep suspicion of anything remotely foreign, including, or perhaps particularly, people with skin any darker than his own. The last time, and Daniel swore it would be the last time, that he had been invited to the Barlings' house, the after-dinner entertainment had consisted of several hours of home video footage of Len water-skiing through various overseas postings. His wife, Jackie, who had bulging eyes and a weakness for chunky costume jewellery, had sat at Len's feet throughout the show making appreciative clucking sounds each time there was a close-up of Len in his micro-trunks. Daniel had made his excuses and left when they reached Dubai, and Len had announced that you had to watch your backs around Arabs. All ruddy queers.

Daniel sat down and opened the envelope. He looked forward to his mother's letters, which managed to blend domestic trivia, family news and world politics with thinly veiled concern for his happiness. He glanced through it to find out how long it would take her, this time, to get to that bit. There were a few lines about his father's imminent retirement, his sister's raging hormones, and his mother's involvement with a new Amnesty International campaign. Then a bit of news about their wider family.

> *I met Lucy's boyfriend the other weekend when we went to see Aunt Emily and Uncle Jack. He's called Joe Redmond. Seemed a nice chap. Very original dress sense. He was wearing a shirt made of material with the Pope on it. Your father was quite taken with it. We got talking and he told me that his parents live in Tiokunda. Small world! Apparently his father is something with the British Council. He said – rather ominously, I thought – that you would be unlikely to forget him if you'd met him.*
>
> *Your great-aunt Eleanor rang this evening. She's staying somewhere near Worthing – visiting an old chap she knew out in Nigeria. He's in some kind of home now, apparently. I must say she*

*didn't sound too good. When I dropped in on her
a few weeks ago she seemed somehow older – very
tired, I thought. And she was always such a tough
old thing. I used to think she'd outlive us all, but
I'm not so sure about that now.*

Daniel swallowed. The thought of great-aunt Eleanor's
dying was as unbearable as it was inevitable. She must be
getting on for eighty-five. He remembered sitting on
her lap as a small child and running his fingers over her
wrinkled face or joining the dots of the liver spots that
covered her hands. He used to spend hours looking at all
the treasures she had brought back with her from Nigeria
– the intricate thorn bush figures, leather amulets to ward
off evil, the Benin bronzes, the round clay pots. He must
write to her again. See if she was serious about visiting
him. Ah! Here it was.

*Your father and I went to a concert in Oxford on
Saturday. I hope you don't mind, but really it would
have been rude to refuse the composer's invitation.
I could tell you that the last piece was dedicated
"to Daniel" and I could even draw some inferences
from that, but you'd just say I was meddling so I
won't. But I really hope that you are happy, my
love, and that you feel you made the right decision.
You know you could always write to—*

Daniel jumped as two fat little hands covered his eyes.
"Guess who, gorgeous?"
"Len! And I thought you didn't care. Must be my
lucky day."

"Oooh, Daniel, you're such a tease." Sandra leant over his shoulder and slid her hands down his chest. "Who's Lucy then?"

"I didn't know that speed-reading was one of your many skills."

"If it's skill you're after," Sandra whispered, her hot breath in his ear, "I'm all yours."

"Wouldn't that be interpreting staff training rather too literally?" Daniel peeled Sandra's hands off him. "It'd be a nice change from Microsoft Excel, though. I'll definitely give it some thought."

"You do that, sweetheart. Now I'm sure I had something to tell you before I was overcome by lust. Oh yes, the boss wants you to do something about that co-funded project in Brikaba. Check out that orange file there. It was the last thing your predecessor did before they recalled him to London. Well, almost the last thing. But I won't go into that sordid matter. It's not for ears as delicate as yours."

Daniel removed Sandra's fondling fingers from his ear and squeezed them affectionately.

"When?"

"What about my place, eight o'clock?"

"I mean when does he want me to go?"

"He didn't say. A call came through from the visa office and he suddenly went all preoccupied on me. Can't think why," she added with heavy irony. "Anyway, I'll love you and leave you."

As she shut his door, Daniel's face lit up with triumphant relief.

"Miss Piggy! That's it. Thank God!"

"Sort these, could you," said Kamal, slapping a pile of invoices down on Rachel's desk.

She pushed them to one side without looking up from her book.

"Now, please. Is it really too much to expect—" Kamal stopped abruptly as he noticed a large woman in an elaborate headdress fingering swathes of felt appliqué. He walked up to the woman, smiling broadly, his arms outstretched. "Ah, Mrs N'Jie. It's been too long. How are you? And the family?"

"All fine. All fine. And yours?" answered Mrs N'Jie, clearly delighted to find Kamal in the shop.

"Very well indeed." Kamal glanced at Rachel, who had not moved.

Mrs N'Jie prodded Kamal's chest with a podgy finger. "And you, Kamal. We haven't seen you since Yassin's wedding. You must come round. We want to show you the photographs. Such beautiful outfits, all of them. You were really too, too generous."

Kamal waved his hand dismissively. "It was a pleasure. What can I do for you today? Your timing's perfect, you know. Our new shipment of Japanese voile is about to arrive. I'll show you the samples." He steered her towards the back of the shop and up the stairs towards the office. "How's Tunde? I hear he's been having discussions about a new timeshare. With some British entrepreneur. Tell him to drop by when he can get away from the Ministry. Better make it soon, though. I'm going to be away buying in China for two months.

"Rachel," he called over his shoulder, "get two

Cokes and bring them up here. Quickly, please. I'm sure the Minister's wife must be thirsty in this heat." He shut the office door.

Rachel put on her sandals and got up. In front of her stood a middle-aged man. He had wispy, thinning, reddish hair through which his scalp glistened with tiny beads of sweat. He was dressed in a pair of faded blue cotton trousers, leather open-toed sandals and, Rachel noted, a short-sleeved shirt from which beamed recurring faces of Pope John Paul II. She felt the corners of her mouth twitch.

"I know," the man said, shrugging his shoulders and grinning. "I look like a sad bastard. But I love it." He performed an elegant twirl. "Joseph and your many-coloured coat – just eat your heart out. It's why I came, actually. The friend who gave me this gorgeous garment said you had more. I've come to the right place, haven't I?" He unravelled a small scrap of paper. "H. A. Sharif and Sons?"

"Second aisle along. Next to the Virgin Mary polyester."

"The Virgin Mary? I think I must have died and woken up in heaven. I knew it had to happen one day. Forty years in the bush and finally my reward. God! Sister Mary Philomena will be in ecstasy! She's not stopped going on about this shirt since Isabel sent it. She was right. This place is a treasure trove."

He looked directly at Rachel and smiled. His face was open and friendly, pale and freckled. His voice had a slight Irish twang. He walked down the second aisle.

"Perfect!" he called. "I'll have four metres of Our Lady and four of His Holiness, if you please."

As Rachel cut the cloth, she remembered selling the Pope John Paul material to a plump, chatty woman who had chuckled as she bought it – had said it was for a priest friend. Rachel looked up at the customer. He had his back to her and was stroking the rolls of damask, tracing his fingers round the intricate, raised patterns.

"It's all so beautiful. I can see why a person would want to surround themselves with cloth."

"I hate it."

"What was that, my dear?" said the priest, turning to her.

"That's seventy-five lamasi."

"Well, feck me." He took out a damp roll of notes from his pocket and carefully peeled them apart. "It soon adds up, doesn't it? Still, worth it for the beatific smile that will suffuse the face of the lovely Sister Mary Philomena and keep me in decent meals for a good while. Our sartorial elegance will be the talk of Brikaba."

"Brikaba?" Rachel raised her eyebrows.

"That's the response I get from most of you city dwellers. But you don't know what you're all missing. There's something strangely beautiful about hundreds of miles of scrub. At least that's the story I'm sticking to. Anyway, tell me, why do you hate all this?" He gestured at the piles of cloth.

"I don't think you'd want to know," said Rachel, taking the money from him.

"I might. We old bush priests lead a quiet life."

Rachel looked at him. He had pale blue eyes surrounded by fine wrinkles. She realised that he could be in his sixties. There was something about him that made her hesitate to pick up her book. She felt a curious lightness. She tried, and failed, to remember the last time she had felt anything like this.

"That's not what they say down here."

The priest laughed. "Well, some of us don't, for sure. But you wouldn't want to know about that."

She smiled. "I might."

The priest laughed again. "It'd take too long. You'd be middle-aged by the time I'd got half way. I'd be administering the last rites by the time I'd brought you up to 1974."

"They'd be wasted on me. Have you really been a priest there for forty years?"

"Forty-two years next July."

"Always in Brikaba?"

"There, or fifty miles north, in Kamina. And briefly in Nigeria. Why, do you know it?"

"I went to Brikaba once – Kamina too."

"Did you now? And why was that, then?"

"Just visiting."

"Only, visitors are quite an event up there. I'm surprised I didn't hear about it. Most strangers end up in the Mission compound at some point and few go away without a bottle or two of Sister Mary Philomena's brew."

"I didn't stay long." Rachel swallowed and looked away for a moment.

"Well, if you come again, be sure to ask for Father Seamus. They all know me. And I can guarantee a cold beer and a warm welcome – and a bottle of the sister's best, of course."

"Thank you," said Rachel. She handed him the package. "I don't drink. But the welcome sounds good."

"Be sure not to forget, now?"

"I won't. Brikaba Mission compound. Not too hard to remember."

"Goodbye then."

Father Seamus tucked the package into a frayed cotton bag and walked towards the door. He turned at the grille.

"I never asked your name. You see what happens to a man's manners after too long in the bush."

"Rachel."

"Rachel Sharif?"

"No. Rachel Kayne."

"Well, Rachel Kayne." He hesitated a moment. "Be sure and look us up now. I'll take it as a personal slight if I ever hear you were up there and didn't call by."

He turned again and walked out into the sunlight. Rachel felt the sense of lightness evaporating into the still, hot air.

"I asked you to get two Cokes. You obviously got sidetracked. Who's your new friend?"

She did not look up.

"I said, who's your new friend?"

"What friend?"

"Your friend in the shirt."

"A customer. I sold him some cloth. It's what I'm meant to do, isn't it?"

"You don't normally stand gossiping with the customers. It's as much as you can usually manage to say a few civil words. And you didn't even stretch to that earlier."

"I thought you did the paperwork up in that gallery. And entertained clients, of course. I didn't realise you'd diversified into staff surveillance and on-the-job training."

"Come, Rachel. That tone of voice does not suit you. If I were you—"

Rachel stood up. The wooden chair tipped backwards and crashed to the floor. Her voice was low and angry. "If you were me, I doubt you'd sit selling cloth in this shit-hole all day. I doubt you'd be—"

"I don't think that this is the time or the place for an argument, my darling." He nodded up to the gallery. "Never mind about the drinks now. Just sort these." He pointed at the invoices. "I'm going to the N'Jies' this evening and I expect you to be in a better mood by the time I get home."

Cancun, January 12th 1993

In Mexico for a fortnight
in search of Sun. I'm lying
in a hammock with a book,
thinking of how much
you'd love it here - you
should go for a transfer.
There's a child in the little house behind
this hotel who's adopted ~~us~~ me who reminds
me so much of the lovely Abdulai Jammeh from
Brikaba. Rx

Daniel Maddison
FCO Tiokunda
c/o Ring Charles St.
London SW1A2AH

It was Sunday morning. On the dining-room table lay the residue of breakfast – an open jar of Chivers marmalade, crumbs of toast, the remains of some butter and a half-empty cafetière. Alec and Fenella sat at opposite ends of the long, slightly shabby, teak-effect table while their maid ran a yellow duster slowly and carefully across the areas that were not covered in breakfast debris. As she dusted, the uneven table legs hit the floor with an almost musical regularity.

The dining-room table, along with all the other furniture on the High Commission compound, had arrived flat-packed from Britain and was beginning to revert to its original form. The only solace, Fenella sometimes reflected, was that half the world's embassy wives would be sitting at the same cheap wood-chip rubbish, bought in bulk by the Crown Agents. On bad days, this was little consolation. They didn't all have to put up with a hardship post: the endless burning skies, the garish reds, yellows and purples of the flame trees and bougainvillaea which could bring on a migraine before you knew it, and the ineptitude of the local staff who, quite honestly, should have stayed up in their trees.

"Do you have to do that now, Kaddy?" Fenella asked in a tone of voice that suggested that there was really only one response, and one that should be effected immediately. Kaddy fled to the kitchen without looking up, relieved to be returning to the safety and comfort of the cook, the only member of the domestic staff who had so far avoided Fenella's lashing tongue and hands.

"She was just trying to be helpful," Alec ventured. "I'm not sure that you should be quite so hard on the staff. We seem to be getting through them at a rate of knots."

"Since when have workers' rights been one of your major preoccupations, Mr Nye Bevan?"

Fenella opened up a small enamel pillbox and began to arrange the tablets in order of size at the side of her plate. When she had done this, she gathered them all up and rearranged them by colour, the lightest one at the head of the line.

"Alec, for Christ's sake, don't do that," she snapped, without looking up.

"Do what?"

"Fiddle with the hairs in your nose. It makes me feel sick."

"I wasn't. Anyway, how can you see what I'm doing when you're … what *are* you doing, by the way?"

Fenella scooped up the tablets, tossed them into her mouth and swallowed them with the remains of her coffee. She grimaced.

"Any post for me?" she asked, nodding towards the pile of papers in front of Alec. Why Isatou had to deliver the office post to the residence on a Sunday, Fenella could not imagine. She was probably still sitting in the kitchen, gossiping with the cook who was doubtless some kind of relation. Who wasn't, after all?

Alec started dealing out the envelopes. "One for you. Two for me. Three Christmas cards. A postcard for you. Another Christmas card. *Hello!* magazine, three weeks old, for you."

"Just give me my post." She snatched one of the envelopes from the pile and glanced at the return address. "About time the Brownley-Thomases wrote.

We spent enough on them in London."

"We were staying with them."

"Even so. And I don't think they need have found that hideous poem quite so hilarious."

"What hideous poem?"

"You know. Patrick Redmond's thing in the *London Review of Books*."

"Oh. You mean 'Cocktails at—'"

"Thank you, Alec. I hardly think I need to be reminded of that shoddy little ... little piece of shit."

"Don't you think you're over-reacting just a little bit?" Fenella glared at him. "No," he muttered. "Obviously not. What's that?"

"What?"

"That bit of paper that fell out of the envelope."

Alec walked over to Fenella's end of the table and picked up a small cutting that had fallen into the butter dish. He wiped the butter off on her napkin.

"It's another of Redmond's poems. The Brownley-Thomases obviously realise that you're particularly keen on his writing. You could start a scrapbook. It could be worth a fortune one day."

"Oh, ha ha. You are such a wit, Alec."

"Do you think so?" Alec asked, pleased. "Listen, I'll read it."

"No. Please don't ..."

Alec took a deep breath. "'Cutting the Cloth' ...

"Close your eyes and watch her cut the cloth
Feel crimson velvet slip towards the floor.
Touch, but gently now, the satin of her moon-white
thighs."

He stopped abruptly. "How can you watch something with your eyes closed? The man's more of a fool than I thought. Perhaps he meant 'open your eyes'. How he manages to get anything published is a mystery to me."

"The Catholic Mafia," said Fenella, lighting a cigarette.

"Can't be. The Mafia would want to call it the *Sicilian Review of Books* or the *Neapolitan Review of Books*, wouldn't they? Not the *London Review of Books*, unless it's some kind of cover. Ha! Cover! Get it?"

Fenella took a heavy drag on the cigarette and shut her eyes. "The editor was probably at the same prep school as Redmond. Buggered by the same bent monk after evensong."

"Different style from the last poem," Alec mused.

"You mean less like Betjeman and more like those hysterical women who commit suicide and have a following of screeching lesbians who wail over their graves in ghastly parts of the north."

"Well, not really."

"Well, what then, Melvyn? You're not on the bloody *South Bank Show* now."

"God, your memory's getting bad. First Nye, then Melvyn. Must be all those pills you take."

He held the cutting out in front of him again and continued.

"*Close your eyes and watch her cut the cloth*
Feel crimson velvet slip towards the floor.
Touch, but gently now, the satin of her moon-white
    thighs.
Close your eyes, caress her silken brow ...

"He's used 'close your eyes' before," he said. "You'd think the copy-editors would do a better job than that, even if they are Italian."

"What's it called again? 'Lament in John Lewis's Soft Furnishing Department'?"

"'Cutting the—'"

"No. Don't tell me. I'm really not interested."

The phone rang. They heard Kaddy answer it in the hall. After a while, she came in, keeping literally an arm's length from Fenella.

"Madam, it's for you. Paavo Valjakka from the Finnish Embassy."

"Can't you see I'm busy?" said Fenella. "Say I'll phone back."

"That's nice. Will you be playing bridge today?" said Alec, with delicious realisation that Sunday could be turning out to be rather more interesting than he had anticipated. With any luck, Isatou would still be somewhere in the house.

"I might," said Fenella, trying to keep the excitement out of her voice.

"Is she any good?" asked Alec.

"Is who any good?"

"Paavo Valjakka. You should know. You spend enough time playing bridge with her."

Fenella smiled at Alec. She felt a surge of affection for her poor witless husband.

"Yes, she's not bad. Not bad at all. And good company." Fenella had a sudden idea. "In fact we were thinking of going to a bridge tournament in Dakar. Three days in March. You wouldn't mind, would you?"

Alec smiled at Fenella. "Of course, you must go.

Why don't you stay on for a few days? See the sights – if there are any. I must say, I always think the Finns are a bit cold and fish-like. But if you two get on, that's fine. You probably need your girls' talk."

"We do get on. We get on very well indeed." Fenella picked up her napkin to hide her uncharacteristically enormous smile. Then she went out into the hall to ring Paavo. Kaddy was dusting the telephone table. She noticed that there was a large piece of crumb-encrusted butter stuck to Fenella's cheek. She wondered, briefly, whether to tell her, then decided that it would be safer all round not to.

Rome, August 4th, 1994

In Rome as you can
see - Been here nearly
a year. Studying with
Guido Ansaldi and doing
some teaching. I hear
from my reliable mole
at the foreign office that
you've been transferred to Paris.
Quite a meteoric rise. Perhaps you were right
to make the choice you did. Take care R x

Daniel Maddison
FCO Paris
C/o King Charles St
London SW1A 2AH

D aniel! How lovely to see you. Come on in." Isabel
hugged Daniel. "We've missed you at Bakari's. You
haven't been down to the beach for ages. Patrick was
even talking of venturing onto the High Commission
compound to rescue you from the clutches of old
Alec, which, for Patrick, must be a sign of something
approaching deep affection."

Daniel laughed. "Is he in?"

"He's around but he's in the middle of something.
I'm sure he won't be long. Is everything all right?"

"Yes, I'm fine, I suppose. Though I can't think of
anything remotely interesting to tell you about."

"It's just nice to see you. Here, have a beer."

"Thanks." Daniel held the bottle to his cheek, feeling
the icy drops of condensation on his skin. "Actually, I
do have some news. I'm going up-country in a couple of
weeks. To look at some defunct High Commission funded
project, and as Sandra's tipped me off that the Barlings
are planning a slide show devoted to the renovation of
their gîte in the Auvergne, a week in Brikaba suddenly
seems a very exciting option."

"Brikaba? That'll be nice."

"That's not what most people say when I tell them.
Mostly they just smirk."

"No, well. I suppose it's not everyone's cup of tea,
but if you want to really feel you're in West Africa and
not in a South London suburb that has invested heavily
in tropical flora, you're going to the right place. And you
must look up Father Seamus."

"Who's he?"

"A very old and dear friend of ours. He was down
here a while ago. You may have seen him around town.

A redhead. Sixty-ish. Likes loud shirts. He met your friend."

"Which one?" asked Daniel, realising as he did so that he didn't really have any friends here except Isabel and Patrick. And possibly Sandra Didsbury, if he really wanted to up the numbers.

"Rachel."

"Rachel?"

"He said he had a bit of a chat with her in the shop. I know. I find it hard to imagine too. She didn't seem the chatting kind to me."

"Nor me. What did she say?"

"I don't really know. Said she hated cloth, apparently, which seems a shame if that's what she's surrounded by all day."

For a while neither of them said anything. Isabel got out her sewing. Daniel sat back in the cane armchair and drank his beer.

"I see her all the time," Daniel said, putting the bottle down on the floor and staring out over the veranda wall at the bougainvillaea. "I don't know why." He shut his eyes. "I have this one image. It keeps coming back to me. Like a still from a film. Just her in the shop in a black dress, her hand pushing her hair out of her face, staring straight at me." He opened his eyes and turned to Isabel. "It happened once before."

Isabel looked up from her sewing and waited for him to continue.

"I was in India and Bhutan a few years ago. I'd been travelling for weeks and I'd used up about twelve rolls of film. Come to think of it, maybe I should invite the Barlings round for a return show of four hundred and fifty slides of yaks, snowy mountain peaks, small grinning children and fluttering prayer flags. At least that would guarantee I'd never be invited back. Anyway, I'd got a bit sick of seeing everything through a camera lens, so when I got to Calcutta, I left my camera in the hotel room and just looked. It was amazing. For years, my memories of Calcutta were incredibly vivid. But I've got one memory, one image, that doesn't fade at all."

"A girl?"

"No." He frowned. "A sort of ... sort of freak. There was a young woman sitting on the pavement. She had this child with her. A crowd had gathered round and people were nudging each other and pointing, throwing coins into a tin. I went a bit closer and saw that the child wasn't really a child. At least, I don't think it was. It seemed to have the body of a baby and the head of a much older person. No hair. Naked. The mother was smiling at the child, so proudly, while it just stood quietly amongst the noise of the city and looked out at the crowd. I tried to walk past, and as I did, it looked straight at me. It's that image that has stayed with me – that calm, wise, old face. A face that I couldn't read at all and that I couldn't forget."

For a while, neither of them said anything. Isabel continued to sew while Daniel ran his finger through the condensation on the bottle, watching the drops run down and form a small puddle on the floor.

"Don't ask me what the connection is," he said at last.

"Does there need to be a connection? I think I know what you're trying to say. I've got one or two memories that stand out too." Isabel did not need to shut her eyes to conjure up a much, much younger Patrick, the look on his face at once abashed, guilty and defiant. And lying on the couch behind him, a very young, very beautiful Kanuri woman, wearing nothing but a heavy gold nose ring.

"Where would I find that priest you mentioned?"

"What? Sorry, I was miles away."

"That priest in Brikaba."

"Oh, Father Seamus. At the Mission compound. You can't miss it. Ask anyone."

Isabel and Daniel turned as they heard footsteps.

"Izzy, my adorable muse. And Daniel, too!" Patrick grasped Daniel's hand with both of his. "Where've you been? We were afraid you'd been confined to barracks for fraternising with natives and ne'er-do-wells. How are you, my boy? How long have you been here? Why didn't you tell me he'd come, Izzy?"

"I assumed that you didn't want to be disturbed, my love." Isabel went over to Patrick and kissed him. "Had a good afternoon?"

"Very," he said, putting his arms around her. "Kaddy!" he shouted down the corridor. "Finish putting on your clothes and come and say hello to Isabel. And you can meet our friend Daniel."

A girl of about sixteen came out of one of the back rooms and stood smiling shyly at the door, smoothing down her batik wrapper and blouse.

"Hello, Kaddy, dear," said Isabel. "How are you? And how are all the family? Kaddy, this is Daniel. Daniel, Kaddy. You've got something in common, you know."

"Have we?" asked Daniel, trying to make some kind of sense of the scene.

"The Mosses. One of you works for Alec and the other for Fenella."

Patrick groaned theatrically. "Talk about the devil and the deep blue sea. It doesn't really bear thinking about. Come on, Kaddy. I'd better take you home or your mother will send your brothers out to get me. Don't you dare leave before I get back, Daniel. Resort to whatever devious means you need to keep him here, Isabel. I'll be ten minutes."

Daniel looked at Isabel, trying to read the expression on her face. He looked away and tried out a few phrases in his head. They all sounded completely ridiculous.

When he looked back at Isabel, he saw that she was smiling gently at him.

"Don't worry. It's not what you think."

"I don't really know what I think."

"He just takes photographs. It's a kind of hobby."

"A hobby? Birdwatching's a hobby. Or stamp collecting. That's pornography."

"Oh, Daniel, love. Nothing's that black and white, so to speak."

"But it's … you must mind. Don't you?"

"I used to. Terribly. But that was a very long time ago. The first time we were posted here. It's amazing what you can adapt to."

"But why should you have to?" Daniel asked, angrily.

"Love's a complicated thing. I'd have thought that you, of all people, would know that," she replied kindly. "When it first happened, I thought my world was falling apart. We'd not been in Bakinabe for long. We were way up in the north – near Kamina. I didn't know what to do, or what to think. I left the house and walked into the town – it was no more than a village then. I wanted to get away from everyone – from the crowd of little children who used to follow me everywhere, from the old men sitting under the trees, from the women in the next compound who used to stroke my white skin and laugh, but mostly from Patrick. There was a small church in the square – the early missionaries had really pushed the boat out there – so I walked in and sat down. And I wept."

Daniel felt tears pricking in his own eyes.

"After a while," she continued, "I realised that someone was sitting next to me. A young man, with lots of auburn curls, wearing a bright pink shirt. And so I met Father Seamus, who helped me see that my world hadn't fallen apart, and that love could be truly unconditional if you really loved enough. And it turned out that Patrick and I did love enough then, and we still do now."

"You're amazing," said Daniel.

"Rubbish! I'm a fat old thing, with a husband who wears filthy hats and takes pictures of naked girls. But every day I wake up and thank God for my life, for my children, my husband and my friends. And that includes you, Daniel, whether you like it or not."

In the middle of the river, silhouetted against the darkening sky, a lone fisherman casts his net. It sparkles in the last rays of the evening sun. Thomas Kayne stands at the river's edge. He looks out over the water, to the smoke rising above the round mud houses. It swirls up through the branches of the baobab trees as it disappears into the mauve sky. Scarlet and orange ripples lap against his bare feet, filling the deep crevices in his parched, cracked soles. The water feels like. Like mercury. A hundred and five. A cool hand on his head. Saint Stanley. Caressing. Smooth. Slippery. A slippery kipper. A slippery character. Watch your back. Watch the trap. Clap trap. Eleanor. That's just claptrap. Come here and kiss me, *Ngase*. Fish trap. Fishnet. Watch those ladies of the night, old boy.

He dips his hands into the water, and raises them high above his head. He watches the drops splash back into the river. Again, he scoops up the water and watches it fall – sudden splashes then silent ripples – like the thoughts that burst into his head then diffuse before he can make sense of them. He frowns as he drinks from his cupped hands.

He calls to the opposite bank, calls for the boatman. The fisherman in the river turns to look at the old man and shakes his head. Again, Thomas Kayne calls out. *Toi a wonno sa'I nde mi euni ma?* Where were you when I called? Where were you when I called?

"She's out there, again, Father. Just sitting under that old neem tree. It's a shame, so it is."

Sister Mary Philomena stood looking out of the screen door wiping her wet hands on her brand new polyester apron. The Virgin Mary's cheeks glistened with tears.

"Since when has sitting under a neem tree been a shame?" Father Seamus walked up behind the nun, put his hands on her bony shoulders and followed her gaze. A young woman dressed in knee-length cut-off denim shorts, a worn green T-shirt and a pair of flip-flops was, indeed, sitting under the tree just outside the compound. He sighed, and rolled his eyes up into his head melodramatically.

"Look, I know, more than most, how many plenary indulgences the good Lord would award me for a conversion – and God knows we haven't had any of those since I did a job lot on the Jammeh family in 1969. But I draw the line at unsettled, homesick young volunteers like Susie who have a problem separating real life from *The Thorn Birds*."

Sister Mary Philomena snorted.

"All right, all right. I appreciate I'm no Richard Chamberlain, but you know perfectly well what I mean. All I did was suggest that she should go away and consider whether conversion to Catholicism was what she really wanted. And now won't you look at her."

"Well, she obviously took you at your word, Father. There she is, now. Considering."

"I didn't mean that she should do it here. Every day.

Like some melancholy gnome. God! She should be out there enjoying life. Living it. Not just thinking about it. A miserable Methodist thousands of miles from home is bound to find this place something of a haven, but that doesn't mean that she has to convert for the sake of a decent meal, a cold beer and a game of chess."

"Seamus O'Malley! If the Bishop could hear you. I don't know. Sometimes I wonder about you, sure I do." Sister Mary Philomena untied her apron, her bony fingers struggling with the knot. "I'm going to visit Sukai Touray's new baby at Banataba. I'll see if the poor girl wants to come with me. Seeing as how you're obviously not in the mood to dispense the milk of human kindness."

"Now, that's not fair. I only said—"

"It's all right, you old dog, you. I was only joking."

She squeezed Father Seamus's arm as she passed him and walked towards the compound wall. He watched her pull the heavy gates open, walk nimbly up a steep bank to the neem tree and crouch down beside Susie. He could see the girl first shake her head and then, a little while later, nod and stagger to her feet, wiping the dust off her shorts. As the two women walked up the dirt track and out of sight, he wondered, as he so often did, about these volunteers, posted so far into the bush.

Over the years he had come to know scores of them. They would be drawn to the shade and tranquillity of the Catholic Mission compound, with its neat beds of flowers marked out by white pebbles – Sister Mary Philomena was a dab hand with a pot of paint – and its tall eucalyptus trees. They would come to play chess with him and poker with Sister Mary Philomena, or just to talk over a glass or two of the sister's brew. Many of them had remained in contact for years after they left. God! If he stayed here much longer they'd be getting snaps of grandchildren.

The VSO volunteers threw themselves into their projects with a zeal that the Bishop – bless his cotton socks – would be proud of. Some of them would give up after a few weeks of squatting over communal bowls of rice and vegetables, and long evenings spent alone, watching the moths flutter into their kerosene lamps. Or they would finally tire of being pursued by hordes of small, curious children as they staggered to their pit latrines where the thriving colonies of cockroaches were silent witness to their chronic diarrhoea. Others would crumble under the weight of trying to teach seventy children the rudiments of English or Agricultural Science in classrooms that contained neither blackboard, nor chalk, nor often any furniture. And then there were those who would leave hurriedly after a desperately misjudged fling with a fellow volunteer or local teacher. Thin and drawn, they would all, whatever the cause of their failure, come to the Mission for a final cold beer, leaving behind them their unread novels, their mosquito nets and a lingering sense of regret.

But the ones who did not leave were often quite remarkable. They stayed on, sometimes for multiple contracts, and grew to love the area as much as he did. There were few compounds that did not boast a small Clive or Sandy or Harriet or whoever, named in honour of the much-loved teachers, agriculturalists and nurses who had lived and worked amongst them.

Father Seamus was more wary of the American Peace

Corps in their baggy tie-dyed trousers and threadbare T-shirts. With a few exceptions, they tended to fall into two camps. There were those who appeared to be in the very earliest stages of high level careers in the Foreign Service – for whom their time here would soon be a distant but formative memory. Then there were those who had immersed themselves in the country so deeply that he doubted they would ever again be able to set foot in an American shopping mall without becoming seriously mentally ill. At least a few Americans, Father Seamus consoled himself, would be able to place one other country besides their own on a map of the world.

His musings were interrupted by the sound of an engine stuttering to a halt and stalling. He opened the screen door and walked out into the compound. A Land Rover was parked just outside the gate and a young man he did not recognise was coming towards him, deftly tucking his shirt into his trousers with one hand and waving in greeting with the other in which he was clutching a large plastic bag. Father Seamus opened the gate. The young man held out his hand and smiled.

"Hello. Father Seamus?"

"Indeed it is." The priest shook his visitor's hand and wondered if he ought to know him. He had very dark brown hair and beautiful dark blue eyes with long black lashes. Just a shame Susie had gone. Maybe the sight of this young man would have been able to bring some colour to her cheeks and take her mind from the sacred to the profane.

"Good to meet you. I'm Daniel Maddison. I'm a friend of the Redmonds. I've brought you one of Isabel's fruit cakes." He held up the plastic bag as proof.

"Anyone bearing Isabel's fruit cake is a friend of mine. Come in. You're very welcome. For one terrible moment when I saw that little Union Jack I thought you might be Len Barling. But you're obviously not and we'll thank the good Lord for that."

The two men walked through the compound and into the house.

"Will you have a cold beer?"

"Just some water would be great. Len Barling's surely never been here, has he?"

Father Seamus laughed. "Good God, no. I have it on good authority he doesn't exist in human form outside the confines of the High Commission compound. No, we had a small argument on the golf course in Tiokunda once. To do with the club's dress code, if you can believe it. Here. It's not very cold. Sister Mary Philomena doesn't believe in taking up beer space in the fridge with water."

Daniel sat down and drank the water. He looked round the room. It was cool and clean and almost bare but for a couple of chairs, a table, and a telephone on top of a bookcase containing an eclectic collection of novels and magazines.

"Don't be fooled by that telephone. It hasn't ever worked but Sister Mary Philomena is an eternal optimist. May I?"

Father Seamus pulled the cake from the bag, put it on the table and looked at it lovingly.

"That Isabel," he said. "God! What would we do without her?"

"I don't know."

The priest looked up at Daniel's face and saw that his expression was suddenly very serious.

"Is she well? She seemed in fine form when I was last down at the coast."

"Yes, fine."

"And Patrick?"

Daniel hesitated. "He's fine too."

"That's grand. Now, tell me what you're doing in the wilds of Brikaba without a High Commission entourage and, more to the point, where you're staying."

"I'm not really without entourage. The driver's got some relations in the next village. I said he could stay the night there and I'd drive on. You may have gathered that by the sound of crunching gears and all the stalling. I'm visiting the goat project."

"Ah! The famous British aid funded goat project. The one without any goats. I know it well. A couple of kilometres from the British aid funded chicken project. You must know it. The one without any—"

"Chickens," Daniel interrupted gloomily. "Yes, I'm afraid I do know it. Well, on that note, I suppose I'd better try to get there."

"Stay here, why don't you. Go on in the morning. We've plenty of room and Sister Mary Philomena's cooking is the finest for miles around. Only I suppose that's not saying much when it comes down to it. But stay, do. Tell me all about yourself."

And Daniel, much to his surprise, did.

"Nice day, Stan. Sleep well, my love?" Vera opens Stanley's curtains and looks out into the garden. "It's a bit stuffy in here, isn't it?" she says, raising the sash window. A large bluebottle flies in. "I'll come and get you up in a little while."

Stanley Shea feels something touch his cheek. Flying ants. The boys in the compound are trying to catch them with kerosene lamps and bowls of water. He can hear the boys whoop and call out. He can hear the sizzle of the ants as they fry in palm oil, and the crunch as the boys bite into the crisp, black abdomens. One of them shyly offers him a handful of fried ants. Stanley shakes his head, smiling, not yet knowing enough of the language to decline politely. The boy shrugs, throwing them into his mouth as he does so. Stanley watches the movement of the boy's jaw, the flash of white on black. He puts his hand out and brushes a piece of ant from the side of the boy's mouth, his fingers lingering for a second or two.

Eleanor Cameron comes into Stanley's room, carrying a bunch of white flowers. She has not been able to resist them, amused that in these days of political correctness one can still buy flowers called kaffir lilies. She moves his breakfast tray and arranges the stems in an ugly cut-glass vase, then draws up a chair to Stanley's bed. She touches his hair.

Stanley feels Musa Mohammed's hand on his head as it is gently turned to the left and right. He hears the sound of the scissors as the final stray hairs are snipped off. He breathes in Musa Mohammed's smell of warm sweat and palm oil as the boy trims his moustache; he looks into his dark brown eyes. Then he grips the wrist of his fifteen-year-old house-boy and pulls him towards him. Musa Mohammed looks alarmed, unused to anything but kindness from "Sah". Stanley takes his face between his two pale hands and draws it to his. Stanley's lips part. Then Musa Mohammed understands.

Miss Cameron is sure she sees Stanley's lips move. He looks calm, almost happy. "How are you ..."

" ... *finding it here, Stanley, if I may call you that?" Eleanor Cameron asks, distractedly fingering the stems of the flowers on the table in front of her.*

"It's beautiful," he answers, watching her pull off the dead flower heads and brush traces of pollen from her floral print dress.

"First time anyone's described this country to us as beautiful," laughs Thomas Kayne, pouring a large measure of gin into a tumbler. "All a bit rough and ready, but we like it."

Green eyes. He sees that Thomas Kayne has the most beautiful green eyes. Eyes which look straight at him, clear and penetrating, searching out the secrets in his soul. Stanley Shea swallows.

"You all right, Shea? Look as though you've seen a ghost. Would you like ..."

" ... to go out? We could go into the garden for a while."

As she gets up to look for Vera, she thinks she sees him frown.

Vera manoeuvres him into an ancient wheelchair with a torn canvas headrest, ruffles his hair and kicks off the brake.

"There you are, you two. Don't go doing anything I wouldn't do."

Eleanor Cameron wheels the chair along the linoleum corridor. It smells of urine and disinfectant, and something else she cannot put her finger on. It must just be the smell of old people. She wonders if that is how she smells. She must remember to ask her niece. She pushes the wheelchair down the ramp, through the double doors, and into the garden. She stops by a bench and sits down, listening to the crows cawing in the skeletal trees.

"My great-nephew, Daniel, is in West Africa now. Funny how these things happen." Eleanor Cameron takes Stanley's hand. Suddenly, she is tired of platitudes, of small talk. She is too old, now, for empty pleasantries. "It wasn't an accident, was it? I know what you felt for Musa Mohammed, you know. I knew right from the beginning – when you first moved to the province and brought your house-boy with you." There, she has said it. His expression has not changed. "The evening you told us he was leaving to get married, I felt so sorry for you. We were all there, do you remember? You, me and Tom, celebrating your birthday. And you were being terribly brave about it, saying it was about time too – that Musa Mohammed's family had been putting pressure on him for years. I should have known how awful you were feeling. But I never thought you'd … you'd try to … and I shouldn't have told you about me and Tom then. Not that evening. But I was so happy, I couldn't wait. Even though Tom wanted us to keep our engagement secret for a bit longer."

Eleanor Cameron sees that Stanley Shea is shivering. *Getting married! What about me? shouts Stanley, as*

the man he loves walks away into the darkness. I love
you, he calls out into the night. I thought you loved me.
He goes to the trunk in his bedroom and takes out a
shotgun. He loads it and holds it to the side of his head.
He tries to steady the gun, screws up his eyes. Tom! he
calls one last time. Then pulls the trigger.

Stanley lets out a strange cry as his head jerks to the left. Eleanor Cameron leans towards him and cradles his head in her arms. She kisses his mutilated face.

"My poor boy, my poor, sweet boy."

Stanley Shea's body shakes with silent sobs.

"Musa Mohammed never stopped loving you, you know. I'm sure of that. That's what I wanted to tell you. He called his first son Stanley. And there is another small Stanley in the compound now. Stanley Musa. Two generations. That's something to be happy about, isn't it?"

Vera looks out at the garden from the kitchen window. She sees Miss Cameron stroking Stanley Shea's head. She seems to be kissing him, too. And it looks as though the old man has put his arms round her and is rocking backwards and forwards like a baby.

Alec walked into the bedroom to find his wife sitting on the bed, surrounded by what looked to him like the entire contents of her wardrobes.

"Packing alread—"

"For Christ's sake, Alec! Do you have to creep up on me like some mutant half-wit?" she said, scrabbling about in the piles of clothes for the cigarette that had dropped out of her mouth. "Can't you knock? Or cough or something? Like any normal person?"

"Don't you mean mute?" said Alec, looking behind him nervously before shutting the door.

"What?"

"Mute. Not mutant."

"No I don't, actually." Fenella re-lit her cigarette and dragged on it heavily. "You're home early," she said as she exhaled. "The wheels of diplomacy ground to a halt? Her Majesty's representative in the crotch of Africa run out of little jobs to do? Surely not."

"Far from it. Some very interesting British trade possibilities. There's this chap Bob Newpin—"

"Not now, Alec," she hissed.

"Well, you asked."

"I didn't. And if you mean that fat little man with the teeth who's been around for weeks, sliming up to the Barlings, I really don't want to know." She started making neat piles of pants and bras. "Jackie said he's from Eltham!"

"Well, *she's* from Bromley."

"Exactly."

"Exactly what? And anyway, I thought you played

bridge at seven on Tuesdays."

There was a soft knock at the door. Alec jumped. Fenella looked up from her packing to see Kaddy standing in the doorway, holding a small parcel.

"From the tailor, madam."

"Put it down there, Kaddy," Fenella said, waving her cigarette towards her dressing table.

"And, Mr Alec, sir, Isatou says shall she wait for you here?"

"Er, no. Tell her it's not convenient after all. I'll go over my notes with her tomorrow."

Kaddy turned and left.

"Another outfit, darling?" Alec said quickly.

Fenella gave him one of her looks. "That's a bit keen, isn't it?"

"You know I like to see you looking nice."

"Bringing the work and the secretary home with—"

"Let's see it?"

Alec busied himself untying the string, relieved to be out of Fenella's direct gaze.

"That's a nice little top." He held up the golden cloth that shimmered with slivers of silver thread.

"It's a dress."

"A dress? Well, don't be catching a cold in it. It'll barely cover that lovely pert little—"

"Thank you, Alec," Fenella snapped, snatching the dress from him and folding it into a tiny square. "You really needn't worry your pretty little head. Dakar isn't known for its inclement weather."

"A bit formal, isn't it? For a bridge tournament?"

"What was that urgent work you just had to bring home?"

"Come to think of it, Dakar is a stylish kind of place. It's perfect. That Finnish chum of yours had better look out."

"What?"

"Well, she won't get a look in with you dazzling the crowds, will she?"

Fenella smiled. "Oh, she'll get a look in all right, Alec. You can be quite sure of that."

"Drink?"

"No more than the average Scandinavian. Why?"

"I meant do you want a drink?"

"Well, why didn't you say that in the first place? I'll have a ginsy tonsy and go easy on the tonsy."

As Alec walked down the stairs and into the drawing room, his hand reached instinctively for his chest. Got to watch the old ticker, he thought. Fenella might be pretty stupid but she was not that stupid. A couple more near misses and he could be in the soup – both metaphorically and literally if Fenella had anything to do with it. (Though, come to think of it, he was at a loss to remember the last time he had seen her in the kitchen doing anything more complicated than slicing a lemon.)

Alec loved the drawing room. If he stood with his back against the French windows and blotted out the incessant chatter of the weaver birds and the distant roar of the Atlantic Ocean, he could almost imagine himself in a top drawer embassy in Europe. A few pieces of decent furniture had crept into the room over the years, along with a rather fine Persian rug that his predecessor had left behind for reasons Alec had never been able to find out. There were passable Constable and Sargent reproductions on the walls. On the mantelpiece was a signed photograph of the Prime Minister, clutching a sturdy handbag, smiling reassuringly from the door of Downing Street. Alec crouched down in front of the drinks cabinet. He took out a bottle of gin, held it up to the light, and frowned.

"Kaddy, bring in some ice and lemon, will you?" he called. "And another bottle of Gordon's."

His knees clicked loudly as he stood up. He walked over to the French windows and looked out over the cliff-top garden with its bright green lawn, its palm trees and beds of tropical plants. To the right of the garden, far beyond the sturdy gate patrolled by a uniformed guard, was a narrow path that led along the top of the cliffs and then plunged down to the beach that lay hidden out of sight below. If he screwed up his eyes, he could make out the shapes, but not the faces, of the people who were making their way to the beach. Traffic was light this evening, Alec mused. A couple of tall local boys off to try their luck with whichever tourists they could charm into an hour or two of energetic sex followed by an eternity of letters begging for marriage, financial support, or a pair of Nike trainers. That fat white couple he saw most evenings that he bothered to look out at the view. A thin woman in a black dress.

"My drink ready yet?" Fenella walked in and threw herself onto the sofa.

"Not quite," he said as he watched the couple stop and stand back to let the woman in black pass them.

"What are you doing? Counting the twitchers?"

"No, actually. I'm just watching people walking down to the beach. What is it about you and birdwatchers?"

"Ridiculous little people who'd be trainspotting if

they were back in Crewe, with their horrible sandals and socks. Sad bastards who think that the possession of *Birds of West Africa*, a pair of binoculars and the ability to reel off a few fancy Latin names makes them into some kind of Richard bloody Attenborough."

"David."

"It's Fenella, you moron. We've been married for nearly thirty years. One would think you'd know that by now."

"It's David Attenborough, I think you'll find."

"Does it really matter?"

"It probably does to David. Ah, Kaddy. Good girl. Put the tray down there."

"About time too!" said Fenella. "What were you doing? Harvesting the sloes? Colouring in the label with a teeny-weeny felt-tip pen?"

"Madam?" asked Kaddy, looking nervously towards Alec for guidance.

"That's fine, Kaddy. Run along now." Alec went over to the drinks cabinet and poured out a double gin and tonic. He handed it to Fenella.

"We ought to walk over the cliffs sometime. You know, down to the beach for a drink," said Alec.

"You can't be serious?" said Fenella as though she had just been asked to urinate into her gin.

"No, well, perhaps not. Well, here's to your trip to Dakar. Let's hope it's a good one."

"Oh it will be, Alec. It will be."

Isabel held a match to the lamp, waited for the familiar plop as the gas ignited, then adjusted the flow until the mantle glowed white. She much preferred the hiss of the gas lamp and the flicker of candlelight to the relentless throb of the standard issue generator that stood, unused, in a small shed in the garden.

She placed the lamp on the veranda table, and sat down heavily on the sofa. There was a sharp crack. Reaching under her thigh, Isabel retrieved half a pencil and a crumpled ball of paper. Further fumblings revealed a mango stone, a rather dirty handkerchief and the other half of the pencil. She smoothed out the paper and held it close to the gas lamp.

If only you had stopped to speak
That day above the darkening sea
We might have seen the girl behind
The widow's weeds, the lock and key.

"Rather Thomas Hardy, isn't it, Paddy?" she called out.

"Rather Thomas who? Ouch! Buggery!" replied Patrick as he stubbed his toes against the doorframe. "Blasted power cuts! These long dark evenings don't half play havoc with my extremities."

"It's not like you to complain," said Isabel, her hand involuntarily reaching for her still pink-flushed neck.

"I didn't mean that particular extremity of mine which has no complaints. No complaints at all," he said, stooping to cup his hands gently round her head and kiss her on her forehead. "I thought I'd got rid of that." He took the piece of paper from Isabel, screwed it back up into a ball and threw it in the direction of the bin. It missed.

"'Widow's weeds'?" said Isabel. "Being surrounded by so much bright cloth all day would probably drive anyone to black. And 'girl'."

"Well, youngish woman of indeterminate age wouldn't have scanned, would it?"

"And what lock and key? She looked pretty free to me that evening. And I don't remember noticing that she was chained to the floor when I went into her shop."

"It's not like you to be so literal, Izzy."

"No, I know. I'm sorry, my love. It's just that someone around here has to retain some kind of normal response to things."

"Meaning what, exactly?"

"Well, first Daniel and now you. Even Father Seamus."

"Even Father Seamus what?"

"Asked after her in his last letter."

"If I didn't know you better, Isabel, my old girl, I'd think you were jealous."

"Well, you do and I'm not. And while we're on the subject of strange obsessions, didn't you say that Isatou was coming to sit for you this evening?"

"She was, but she sent a note round earlier with Baboucar to say she wasn't feeling well. I can't say I'm surprised – working for old Alec would be enough to make anyone ill."

"I'm really not sure that he merits the amount of scorn you insist on pouring on him. Just because he once had the temerity to ask if you ever did any English language curriculum development or just sat in a beach bar all day writing doggerel. At the end of the day he does hold the purse strings, you know."

"Isabel! Whose side are you on?" Patrick looked at his wife with a genuinely hurt expression.

"There are no sides, Patrick, but if there were, I'd be on yours, of course, as always. But a) he was plastered, b) it was at least two years ago that he said it and c) when did you last do any curriculum development? Now come here, stop moaning, and let me rub that extremity for you."

Patrick's expression metamorphosed from righteous indignation to unfettered delight. Isabel smiled at him indulgently.

"I meant your foot, my dear."

"It's not my foot that wants stroking," said Patrick.

"No, I know. It's your ego."

"It's not. Come here and I'll prove it."

"I think you proved that quite adequately about half an hour ago. Now why don't you go and do some of that curriculum development you're apparently so keen on. You can take this lamp with you. I like sitting here in the dark. Or go and buy some more candles. I heard it from a reliable source that there are going to be a lot more of these power cuts in the next few weeks."

Patrick grunted, and walked out into the street, limping theatrically. On the corner was a tiny wooden kiosk eerily lit by a paraffin lamp which balanced precariously on the edge of one of the tightly packed shelves that was home to myriad batteries, tins of condensed milk, cigarettes, sticks of bread, matchboxes and paper cones of sugar. Patrick peered over the counter. Squatting on the floor of the booth, swathed in blue robes, and smoking cheroots, were two Mauritanians. The older of the two rose gracefully to his feet, re-tying his turban as he did so. He looked at Patrick, his fine, dark features expressionless in the dim light. Patrick nodded a greeting and gestured towards the packets of candles on the top shelf. It occurred to him that though this man had been the subject of one of his better poems now immortalised in Faber's best-selling poetry anthology of 1989, he knew almost nothing about him. He'd be hard pressed to make a sensible guess at the capital of Mauritania, let alone where this man lived; had no idea what he did when not holed up in this kiosk, and what he really thought about. And who was the other man? His son? Brother? Lover? A fragment of Virginia Woolf drifted into Patrick's mind as he handed over a note, took the candles and waited for his change. *And this, Lily thought ... this making up scenes about them, is what we call 'knowing' people, 'thinking' of them, 'being fond' of them!* It was all Isabel's and that black-clad cloth-woman's fault, he thought grumpily. He wrote poems, for goodness' sake, not historical biographies. There was nothing wrong in poets delving into the lives and souls of complete strangers and drawing out the gossamer threads of a poetic truth for their own creative ends. Was there?

Patrick was surprised to see a smile light up the Mauritanian's face as he handed over the coins. As Patrick smiled back, he realised that the smile was directed not at him, but to someone standing behind him. He turned and found himself staring into the face of the subject of his recently aborted poem. He opened his mouth to speak to her but she was already involved in a discussion with the Mauritanian, who was reaching up to the shelves and placing bread, sugar and matches on the counter. He hovered to the side of the kiosk until the transaction was done and she turned back to her car.

"It's Rachel, I believe? You've already had the pleasure of meeting my wife, Isabel. Here, in fact. A while back. And in your shop." He held out his hand. "Pope John Paul II."

Rachel hesitated.

"No, I think I'd better start that again. It's Patrick Redmond. John Paul II is the cloth we've been buying from you in abundance. And the Pope too, of course."

Rachel gave a slight smile and took his outstretched hand.

"And you passed us on the cliff path a few days ago," Patrick continued. "We looked for you on the beach when we got down there but you'd vanished."

He could see from her impassive gaze that it was very unlikely that Rachel was going to explain her disappearance, or indeed say anything else at all. She took her car keys out of her pocket.

"That was very impressive. Your Bakawa, I mean," he persisted. "You must have studied it."

"No. I just picked bits up. Over the years. And a lot of that conversation was in Arabic actually. Which I did study once."

"Really?"

"A long time ago."

"An unusual choice of language. Look ..." said Patrick, realising that she was about to get into her car, and wanting to know more. "Why don't you come in for a drink?"

119

Rachel looked across to the Redmonds' house. She hesitated, almost, it seemed to Patrick, as though she was trying to remember the vocabulary of acceptance. Then, suddenly and with a palpable tremor, the electricity shuddered back to life. The house lit up like a cruise ship sailing off through the night. As though rousing herself from a dream, Rachel shook her head.

"No. Thank you. It's very kind of you. But I'm expected back."

"Perhaps another time?"

"Yes, perhaps."

Patrick watched as she got into her car and drove off, then walked back towards the house, his damaged foot forgotten.

Rome, March 4th 1995

Would you believe me
if I said I had run
into Father Seamus
from Brikaba in St Peters
square yesterday?
I recognised the shirt before
I recognised the priest. I don't know which of
us was more surprised to see each other.
He's here as part of a delegation of missionary
priests to the Vatican. We only had a few minutes
to talk - a pity. R x

Daniel Mastolison
FCO Paris
c/o King Charles St
London SW1A 2AH

B ob Newpin was having a bad day. It had started with the incident at the petrol station, when some native chap in a ripped Michael Jackson T-shirt had engaged him in a complicated conversation about favourable exchange rates while his accomplice had deftly removed his briefcase through the passenger window. This was followed by the police inquiry which had consisted of Newpin sitting for two hours on a wooden bench in the police station while a desk sergeant made laborious notes on scraps of paper with a foot-long novelty pencil tipped with a large pink tassel.

As if this were not bad enough, the prisoners in the two filthy cells directly opposite the bench had kept up a running commentary in some strange language that was very definitely not English, scraping their tin cups across the bars and occasionally bursting out into peals of helpless laughter. Finally, having explained to the sergeant very loudly, very clearly and very often that there was about as much chance of his handing over the money to fill the police car with fuel to enable a search of the area to take place as there was of his finding someone who was not a complete moron in this hell-hole of incompetence, imbecility and inefficiency, Newpin had left.

Desperate for a drink to steady his frayed nerves, he walked across to the one decent café in the town. Situated on the first floor of an old colonial building, with wooden tables and red and yellow umbrellas set out along a balcony overlooking the street, it boasted a good view of the market and the river, and a reputation for satisfying the cravings of homesick expatriates. Bob Newpin looked over the menu at his fellow diners. A bunch of dirty squatter types who appeared to be sharing a banana pancake, and an obvious nutter in a grey canvas hat sitting at a table covered with books and papers who kept looking up at him and then writing in his little black notebook. Where did the normal people hang out in this city?

"Hey, Susie, over here," one of the squatters called out as a sallow-faced young woman walked in, her worn flip-flops dragging on the floor. "Grab yourself a fork!"

"No thanks, I'm not hungry." Susie pulled up a chair and joined the group.

"Still full of the Holy Spirit?" one of them asked, his mouth crammed with squashed banana. "A surfeit of manna from heaven?"

"Oh ha bloody ha, you're such a wit, Neil. Must be why the mosquitoes love you so much," Susie replied, kicking him hard on one of his bite-infested ankles.

"Any parties tonight?" another of them asked. "About time old Alec put on another bash."

"Not heard of any. Think we can all crash at Maggie's?"

"No problem. It's her penalty for having running water and electricity."

Bob Newpin ordered a beer and turned to look at the view from the balcony. A couple of shifty-looking Arabs in blue robes and turbans were pissing into the storm drain while an emaciated dog snuffled at the remains of what looked like a dead rat. A sight for sore eyes and definitely not one for his timeshare clients. That was for sure.

A young man, clutching a small parcel, walked along the road, dodging the urinating Arabs and the rat, which had been abandoned by the dog and was now scattered in several bloody pieces. Newpin stared down at the man. It was that AIDS bloke from the Embassy, Newpin was sure of it.

"Here, Damian! Up here, mate!"

Everyone looked over or up at Newpin except the young man, who appeared not to have heard him and strode on along the edge of the storm drain, round the corner and out of sight.

Fuck and bugger it, thought Newpin as he drained his beer. He could have done with a good chinwag with someone he had something in common with. And that Damian had seemed a good bloke. He put some money on the table and glanced over at the man with the hat, who caught his gaze and held it disconcertingly for a few seconds before returning to his scribbling. Newpin looked at his watch. He had an appointment with Len Barling in half an hour. If he went now, he might be able to persuade the voluptuous Sandra Didsbury to give him a cup of coffee. And he reckoned that was not all he could persuade her to give him. A woman who paraded her assets as she did was most likely up for anything. And he could swear blind that she had winked at him the last time he was there. That, or she had something in her eye. Hard to tell with all this dust.

As Bob Newpin got up to leave, the young people, obviously fortified by their pancake, were getting noisier.

"Well, have you, Susie?"

"Don't be an idiot. He's a priest, isn't he."

"So?"

"What do you mean so? Haven't you heard of celibacy?"

"Not personally, no."

"Oh yeah? So when did you last have any?"

"Any what?"

"Yorkshire pudding. Sex, you idiot."

"That's for me to know and you to merely speculate."

"Hey, Karen. What's the matter with you? Where are you going?"

"Leave her, Dave."

"Why? What's the matter with her?"

"She's got a crush on you, you dick-head."

"You're kidding? I thought she was sleeping with Matthew."

"She was. Then he got off with Hélène Smets at the High Commission party."

"You're joking. That EC guy's wife? She must be at least ten years older than him!"

Bob Newpin could still hear them laughing and talking as he stood on the cracked pavement below the balcony. Bloody hippies. He crossed the road and hailed a taxi. It was as he was getting into it that he felt something soft and rather disgusting under his shoe.

Sandra Didsbury's office door was slightly ajar. Daniel tucked the paper parcel under his arm and raised his hand to knock. Then he hesitated and listened for a moment.

"Come on love, I can see you're gagging for it."

"High time you got your eyes tested, then. Now, if you'll excuse me, I've got work to do and you've got an appointment with Len Barling as you may recall."

"Just one. Go on."

"I'd rather have my face walked over by a swarm of blister beetles, but thanks anyway."

"You ladies! Always playing hard to get. But you can't fool me."

Daniel opened the door and walked in. Sandra was standing over the photocopier studiously avoiding the lascivious gaze of Bob Newpin. She glanced round at Daniel, raising a finely plucked eyebrow to the ceiling as she did so.

"Damian! My main man!" said Newpin. "Saw you in town earlier. Been shopping?" he continued, eyeing Daniel's parcel.

"There's a terrible smell in here," said Daniel, wrinkling his nose.

"It came in with him," said Sandra, still keeping her back to Newpin.

"Now, now, no need to get personal." Newpin sounded rather hurt. "Big fine girl like you ought to be able to take a compliment."

"Less of the big, thank you very much."

"What's that on your shoe?" asked Daniel.

Newpin lifted up his foot. Something red and offal-like was hanging from the sole of his desert boot.

"Bugger it! Thought I trod in something."

For a moment, his foot hovered in the air.

"Don't even think of wiping it on my carpet," said Sandra without looking round.

"Women! Eh? Can't live with them. Can't live without them." Newpin sighed as he hopped towards the door. "Beer, sometime, Damian? Ciao!"

Sandra turned and threw her arms round Daniel theatrically.

"Oooh! You're my knight in shining armour, Danny boy. That man's like some kind of leech, but without the subtlety."

"What does he want?" Daniel peeled her arms from around his neck.

"Sometimes I wonder how you passed those Foreign Office exams." Sandra flounced theatrically to her desk and perched on the edge, her little legs swaying like a pair of pork sausages.

"I meant what does he want here – with Len?"

"He's still on about timeshares. In Brikaba."

"Brikaba? I knew about the timeshare idea. But Brikaba! Has the man been there? It's in the middle of nowhere."

"Is it?" Sandra glanced at the map on the wall. "I see what you mean. Anyway – what can I do you for?"

Daniel had practised nonchalance on his way back from town, but he knew, with a sinking feeling, that whatever he said, and however he said it, he would probably sound ridiculous.

"I just wondered – just for interest, you know – is there some kind of list or something – of all the British nationals living here?"

"There might be. Why?"

"Oh, nothing. I just wanted to look someone up."

"Oh yes?" Sandra fixed him with a coy stare. "And who might that someone be?"

"Someone I – look, Sandra, just tell me where it is."

"Say that again. I love it when you come on all masterful."

"I'll give you this." Daniel held out the paper package.

"Oh, that's nice," she said, unwrapping a metre of orange chiffon. "And it's not even my birthday, you naughty boy."

The phone rang. Sandra picked it up. As she listened, Daniel glanced around the office, wondering what a Register of British Nationals might look like. When she put the phone down, her expression had changed.

"You all right?" he asked her.

"I'm fine. But I'm not sure his lordship is. He sounded very odd. A bit shaky, not his usual self. Normally when Fenella's away he goes all jolly on me. Must be missing her (I don't think). Anyway, he wants me in his office. Pronto." She checked her lipstick in her reflection on the framed photograph of her small chubby nieces. "It's over there, if you're still interested." She nodded at a box file on top of the filing cabinet as she walked out of the room. "And don't you go messing it up, Danny boy. Or else."

Daniel took the box and sat down at Sandra's desk. He flicked through the cards, knowing as he did that it was hopeless. She was hardly likely to have registered at the High Commission. No. He was right. There was no Rachel Kayne. He must have been mad to have even thought of it.

"Found what you were after?"

Daniel jumped. "Christ! Sandra! I didn't hear you come in."

"Well I'm not supposed to knock on my own office door, am I?"

"Sorry. I didn't mean that. That didn't take long. Are you OK? You look – I don't know – out of sorts."

"Yes, well. You try dealing with old Alec when he's like that."

"Like what?"

"In a foul mood. Just because I couldn't give him the name of a good local doctor. Then when I pointed out that we have our own doctor here, I thought he'd burst a blood vessel."

"Did he look ill?"

"Not really. Just sort of slightly frantic. Come to think of it, though, I don't think the symptoms show on the face for ages."

"What symptoms?"

"You know." Sandra pointed at Daniel's groin.

Daniel laughed. "Come on, Sandra. Give the man a break! Look – let's live dangerously and go for a shawarma at that filthy café on the corner. I'll treat you to some smoked salmonella."

"How could I refuse an invitation like that?"

"There's just one thing."

"I knew there had to be a catch."

"The name Rachel Kayne doesn't mean anything to you, does it? A British national. Not registered here, though."

"Tut tut! Naughty girl! Rachel Kayne?" Sandra frowned. "No, never heard of her. Should I have?"

"No. It doesn't matter."

"There's a Thomas Kayne, though."

"I didn't see that in the box file."

Sandra laughed. "No. Well, he wouldn't have registered. He's GN."

"He's what?"

"GN. Gone Native."

"Meaning?"

"Like I said before. You sure you passed those exams? Gone Native. You know – No Longer One of Us. No forwarding address. Don't Send Invite to Queen's Birthday Party. That kind of thing. Actually, I don't know if he's still alive. Or ever was alive, come to think of it. He's a bit like the Loch Ness monster. Everyone's heard of him (except you, of course, why doesn't that surprise me) but hardly anyone's ever seen him."

Daniel glanced at Alec's office as they walked towards the foyer.

"Give me a minute, Sandra. Here." He fished a crumpled ten lamasi note out of his pocket. "I recommend the chicken shawarma."

Sandra took the money. "Any more than a minute and I'll give it to the café dog. You have been warned."

Daniel knocked on the door. There was no reply so he pushed it open. Alec was sitting at his desk, his head in his hands. Daniel coughed. The High Commissioner looked up, his face pale and strained, his eyes bloodshot.

"Yes?"

"Can I get you anything?"

"I doubt it." Alec stared past Daniel.

"I'm just going out to lunch. Can I bring you anything back?"

Alec tried to smile and tapped his forehead. "Out to lunch. Oh, I've just been there. Out to lunch and a bit further as well. Anything else you wanted?"

"No. Not really. I'll see you later at the EC do."

Alec did not reply.

"It's at the Smetses' house."

"Send my apologies, will you? There's something I need to sort out."

Daniel wondered, briefly, about asking him whether he had heard of Thomas Kayne but this was clearly not the moment to do so. Something was up. Daniel had known Alec to be oafish and brusque, but never pre-occupied and given to obscure utterings. Nor had Alec ever been known to miss a party, particularly when Fenella was away, and even more particularly when Hélène Smets, with her eclectic and unpredictable choice of guests, was hosting.

Daniel left the room, closing the door quietly behind him, and walked out of the High Commission. Inside the café, with its juddering air-conditioner and fly exterminator that crackled and spat as the insects flew to their electric deaths, Sandra was eating her shawarma. Greyish mayonnaise was dribbling down both sides of her chin, a piece of partly chewed, bruised lettuce was stuck to one of her front teeth and a small chunk of what could have been any kind of animal, or indeed insect, had fallen into her cleavage. With her free hand she was wafting away the flies that were hovering above Daniel's meal.

"Youff jst mishddd smone."

"I've what?"

Sandra swallowed. "You've just missed someone.

Nice chap – not my type, though. Never could fancy a redhead." She took another bite and chewed noisily. "Still, another year in this place and I'll probably have lowered all my standards and ginger-tops in Virgin Mary shirts with a taste for dodgy fast food will have me going weak at the knees."

"Sounds like you've just met Father Seamus."

"Ooh, a priest! I like a challenge."

"I know you do," said Daniel, smiling, as he levered the shawarma into his mouth.

It was hot in Brikaba. Rachel wiped a trickle of sweat from her eye with her bare arm and looked around her. Nothing much seemed to have changed. Behind her, on the edge of the bus park, the market traders were dismantling their displays and folding up fluorescent acrylic baby clothes and khaki-coloured piles of used shirts and trousers. Flies buzzed around the dismembered goats' heads that lay in crooked rows on the ground, their glazed eyes staring out at her.

If she concentrated hard, she could shut out the noise here, too. Gradually, the crunching of bus gears, the shouts of the drivers, and the harsh cawing of the crows that strutted amongst the debris merged into a uniform hum. She walked slowly through the market, looking for something to drink, a plastic bag of frozen hibiscus water or a bottle of warm Fanta, but everything was being packed up. The traders were already heading along the road towards the town centre, balancing their unsold goods on their heads.

Five years ago there had been a small hotel in the centre of the town, but when Rachel got there she found that it had been replaced by a shell of concrete that blossomed bunches of steel reinforcing rods, and a large sign boasting Brikaba Community Centre. A Gift from the British High Commission. Outside, on a platform under a baobab tree, groups of men were starting to brew *ataaya*. The smell of rice and palm oil wafted up from behind compound walls.

She started to walk towards the platform, then stopped. She knew that she would not be able to summon up either the words or the sentiment that would allow her to accept, with grace, the hospitality she would almost certainly be offered. There would be the inevitable questions about what she was doing here all alone and where she came from, and undisguised curiosity about the husband and many children it would be assumed she had left back at home. Someone might even recognise her.

A flicker of a memory kindled somewhere deep inside her: she is sitting in a compound cradling a small baby. She kisses it on its warm, fuzzy black head then hands it back to its smiling mother. She feels the comforting grip of a hand on her shoulder. She can hear the dull pounding of wood on yam, the sound of enamel bowls being laid out on the ground, the laughter. It is her laughter. Rachel shakes her head. The pictures and sounds stop abruptly.

That priest who came into the shop lived somewhere here. He said that everyone would know where the Catholic Mission was. Rachel looked around. A boy of about ten was watching her intently. He was wearing a pair of voluminous orange shorts tied at the waist with a piece of string, and what looked as though it had once – many years ago – been a woman's floral vest. Confused by a Bakawa-speaking *toubab*, the boy frowned up at her. Rachel repeated her question.

"Ah, the father's house. Come, follow," the boy replied, grinning. "Very good man, our Father who Art. He's teach us English."

He hitched up his shorts and took Rachel's hand. For a moment she stood still as she absorbed the gentle warmth of the boy's small, calloused fingers. He tugged her towards the road.

"Come, madam. You come with me. I will be your guider."

The child walked along beside her, sometimes holding her hand, sometimes darting off to show her something – the direction of his village, the women's vegetable garden that his mother worked in, the road that led to the place where his very good friend Miss Susie lived, the well from which his senior brother had once been rescued when he was a small boy, the place he had found an abandoned kitten.

"And look – here – for you."

The child reached up and tucked a sprig of purple bougainvillaea into Rachel's hair. He gazed at her admiringly.

"Now you are like Queen Diana. With your crown. Do you know the beautiful Queen Diana, in London, England?"

They walked about half a mile through the scrub towards a clump of tall trees, the child chattering the whole way.

"Here is our Mission. You are most welcomed." He pushed open the gate and led her through the neat flowerbeds and up to the screen door. He knocked loudly.

"Abdulai Jammeh! Well I never! I wasn't expecting you today. How are you, now, my boy?" Sister Mary Philomena bent over the child and pinched his cheeks. "I don't know what they're feeding you out there in Banataba, but you must have grown a good four inches since I last saw you. And that can't have been more than a week ago, can it?" She straightened up stiffly. "Who's this come to visit then?"

"She is my madam I found in town. I am her guider."

"You are that, for sure. Good lad. There's some mangoes in the kitchen. Help yourself, why don't you? Now – what can I do for you, young lady?"

"Is Father Seamus here?"

"I'm sorry, no. He went down to the coast just a few days ago. Another of his appointments with the Bishop, God help them both." She held out her hand. "I'm Sister Mary Philomena."

"Rachel. Rachel Kayne."

"Well, come in, Rachel Kayne. Put your bag down there. Can I get you something to drink?"

"Some water. Thank you."

"Sure you won't have something a little stronger? The sun's well and truly past the yard-arm whatever one of those might be."

Rachel shook her head.

"Well, you won't mind if I have a cold beer then? I've had one of those days, so I have. It's like the good Lord knows He's to wait until Father Seamus goes away and then land me with a deal of trouble. Two sick babies needing transporting to the hospital, the car in a hundred pieces, and the generator sounding as though it's not long for the world either. Still, never mind about all that now. You'll be wanting somewhere to stay, then?"

"I thought there was a hotel in town. There was when – but it seems to have gone."

Sister Mary Philomena rolled her eyes heavenward.

"You'll have seen our lovely community centre then. We won't be playing badminton there for a good few years. Come here, sit down. As if there weren't enough white elephants up here. There's a proper herd, so there is. You can hear them trumpeting on a full moon. So you've met our Father Seamus, have you?"

"Just once. He came into the shop."

"Wishing for the cloths of heaven."

Rachel looked at the nun in her simple, light blue cotton dress and white headscarf. Sister Mary Philomena laughed.

"He brought me some wonderful material. I had it made up into an apron. See? Over there. The way he described the shop, it reminded me of that Yeats poem. You know ... What's it called now? 'Aedh wishes for the Cloths of Heaven', whoever Aedh is when he's at home. Or she, indeed. How does it go, now?" She closed her eyes and frowned.

"Had I the heavens' embroidered cloths,
Enwrought with golden and silver light,
The blue and the dim and the dark cloths
Of night and light and the half-light,

"I can't remember how it ends, though."

The nun got up to refill her glass. As she stood with her back to Rachel she heard a whisper.

"I would spread the cloths under your feet:
But I, being poor, have only my dreams ... "

It was so faint that, at first, she could barely make out the words. But then she recognised them. Turning, she saw a look of such unhappiness on Rachel's face that she wanted to take her in her arms and hold her. But there was something almost untouchable about the visitor who continued very quietly:

"I have spread my dreams under your feet;
Tread softly because you tread on my dreams."

Rachel finished speaking and shut her eyes. When she opened them, she looked as composed as before. She put her empty glass on the table and stood up.

"Thank you. It was very nice meeting you."

"Where are you off to?"

"Kamina."

"Not tonight you're not. Nor this week, I shouldn't think. The Kamina bus is well and truly out of action. We may be able to find you some private transport tomorrow. I'll ask around first thing."

"Thank you. But I really shouldn't trouble you."

"Nonsense. I'd be glad of the company. And Abdulai Jammeh here will be glad of a new person to practise his English on." Sister Mary Philomena smiled broadly at the boy who was standing in the doorway munching on a mango stone. "We're hoping you'll get into the High School next year, aren't we? Lovely bright lad like you should get in, no trouble." She turned back to Rachel.

"The Mission is going to pay the fees and he's got an aunt who works in the city who'll look after him. Now don't worry. I won't be asking you a lot of questions. Though I can't promise that Abdulai Jammeh won't ask you a deal of things that aren't any of his business. There is just one thing, though, and then I'll get on and make us some dinner. Kayne, you said your surname was. Would that be as in the old wandering judge? Thomas Kayne?"

Rachel was silent for a few moments, then met Sister Mary Philomena's gaze.

"He's my grandfather."

"Isabel! Mind if I join you?"

Isabel looked up from her novel to see Father Seamus smiling at her, a small brown paper package in his hand.

"Oh, no," Isabel sighed dramatically as she stood up to kiss him. "Not you as well. No prizes for where you've been this afternoon."

"What? Oh, this." He burst into a short, but tuneful, rendition of brown paper packages tied up with strings, these are a few of my favourite things. "Don't you just love Julie Andrews? Well, you know, I just couldn't resist the purple and yellow-swirled fuzz. So very 1970s." He spread the cloth out on the table. "I wonder what they make the stuff out of? Some kind of deadly chemical probably. Certainly nothing that's ever been near a cotton plant."

"Very subtle and understated. It'll do you for the Bishop's dinner. How was Rachel Kayne?"

"Not there. The shop appeared to be staffed by a Lebanese teenager. One of those in the epicentre of the gawky, spotty phase. I asked him where she was but he wasn't very forthcoming. Mumbled something about Dakar. Where's Patrick? You've not managed to ditch the scoundrel at long last?"

"At home. Pacing about like a bear with a sore head. He wouldn't say what was up, so I told him not to come down to the beach until he was in a better mood."

"Good for you!" said Father Seamus with feeling, squeezing her hand. "Ah – here's Daniel."

Isabel's face lit up as she saw him approaching the bar. Then she grimaced. "Patrick was right about something at least. It is an epidemic! So come on, Daniel, show us what you bought."

Daniel kissed her and shook hands with Father Seamus. Then he untied the string. A piece of lavender-coloured damask flopped onto the table.

"Ah! I see you favour the more subtle approach," said the priest. "Well, there's no accounting for taste, is there? Good to see you, Daniel. How are you, now?"

"I'm fine, thanks. And you?"

"Never better. It's not often that I get time alone with the woman of my dreams here."

"I'm sorry. I've interrupted you. I'll sit over there."

"Nonsense!" scoffed Isabel. "He's just joking. I was about to get him a beer. What'll you have?"

"A beer, too. Thanks." Daniel turned to Father Seamus. "You weren't joking, were you?"

The priest smiled. "She's a woman in a million, that Isabel."

They sat watching the tourists on the beach. The ones that came as far as Bakari's Beach Bar fell into two distinct camps. There were the ones who had inadvertently strayed from the guarded patches of raked sand in front of their hotels and were either nervously negotiating their way through the stream of persistent beach boys and vendors, or shouting at them to go away, depending on how long they had been in the country, and how far their good intentions had failed them.

Then there were the travellers who had, with some embarrassment, arrived on cheap package flights but were determined to see a bit of "real Africa". They would strike up friendships with local people, visit them in their compounds, learn to brew *ataaya*, have their hair braided, and sometimes offer to pay school fees for a child or two.

Isabel brought their drinks to the table.

"Thank you," said Daniel. "You know I thought that Rachel in the shop reminded me of the Rachel Kayne I knew at Oxford?"

"No," said Father Seamus.

"It's a long story. We'll fill you in later," said Isabel.

"Well, I couldn't find any reference at the High Commission to a Rachel Kayne. But my colleague, Sandra, mentioned a Thomas Kayne."

"Goodness! Is he still alive?" Isabel asked Father Seamus.

"Very much so. I came across him a couple of months ago when I was visiting a family way out near the river. He was trying to get across but there wasn't a ferry. I offered him a lift but he just shook his head. I think he wanted to carry on walking. Some of those so-called development professionals should try that – they might get to see a bit of the country they're so busy trying to develop. No offence to you, Daniel."

"No, I agree. What does he do?"

"Now? He just walks, mainly. They call him the wandering judge. He's a bit like one of those Indian holy men, I suppose. He sleeps and eats where he can. He doesn't say much and what he does say is hard to follow, but I've a deal of respect for the man."

"Don't they say something terrible happened to him once, which unhinged him?" asked Isabel.

"Well, yes, whoever they is."

"Wasn't there something about a house-boy and some scandal there?"

"That and a hundred other empty theories. You know how fast rumours travel, particularly in places where not a lot happens, which is how you could describe my part of the country if you were being polite. But I don't know about unhinged. I'd call unhinged trying to build a timeshare complex in Brikaba, but that doesn't seem to deter anyone," said Father Seamus.

"You've met Bob Newpin, I take it?" Daniel laughed.

"Not yet. But I've heard all about him. I doubt it'll be long now until I have that pleasure."

"Do you think there could be some sort of connection between Rachel and Thomas Kayne?" asked Daniel.

"I wondered that myself," said Father Seamus. "She seemed to know the area. She'd been to Kamina and Brikaba. But that wouldn't explain what she's doing selling cloth, would it? Though I hear she's in Dakar at the moment."

"Is that what that boy told you? When I asked, I just got a surly shrug."

"Well that's because he knows a customer with taste and discernment," said Father Seamus, folding his gaudy cloth and stuffing it back into its wrapping. "And they've got the same surname, of course," he continued as he poured the beer that Isabel had bought him.

"No – she just looks like someone I knew called Rachel Kayne."

"Well, that's what she told me her name was."

"What? I mean, when?"

"I don't know – when I asked her, I suppose."

"You just asked her?"

"Daniel, dear, I'd be the last person to say anything

approaching I told you so, but I do remember suggesting you ask her what her name was quite some time ago," said Isabel. There was a loud cough.

"Patrick!" she exclaimed. "About time too! I hope you're in a better mood. Come here and be kissed." Isabel stood up and knocked over Daniel's bottle of beer. It foamed over the lavender damask. "Oh, I'm sorry, Daniel. It's ruined. I'm so clumsy."

"That's OK. Don't worry about it. There's plenty more where that came from." He shuffled up to make room for Patrick who sat down heavily and slapped his canvas hat onto the table.

"I didn't mean to snap at you earlier, Izzy, but it's just so stupid."

"What is? Our conversation was interrupted by your rather impressive flounce, as you may remember."

"That was never a flounce."

"Well, whatever it was. I still don't know why you're so upset."

"Isatou's pregnant."

"Is that all?"

"What do you mean 'Is that all?' After all that advice I gave her, not to mention all those condoms. She had a good job – even if she did have to see those morons in the High Commission all day – and now she's lost her chance of promotion, marriage, everything. She'll end up with a whining baby strapped to her back, selling peanuts to tourists."

"You're sounding like Margaret Thatcher, my love. You'd better look out or before we know it, you'll be appearing for sundowners in a blue suit and a handbag. And when did you ever see an African baby whining on its mother's back?"

"Well, if that's your attitude, I'm going for a walk."

"I just don't see what you're so upset about – assuming you're not the father?"

Daniel choked on his beer.

"Very funny," said Patrick. "She won't say who the father is. Some youth with more sperm than sense."

"Well, what then? The pregnancy won't affect your photographs for months. Anyway – it could be a new departure for you. 'Patrick Redmond – The Fecund Years.' "

"That's not like you."

"What isn't?"

"That tone."

"No, I'm sorry." She kissed him on the forehead. "Let's both go for a walk – if the others will excuse us."

Father Seamus and Daniel watched them as they walked along the beach then back up the cliffs.

"You can take that worried look off your face, Daniel. It won't be Patrick who's the father. I'd bet Sister Mary Philomena's last bottle of hooch on it."

Daniel looked embarrassed. Father Seamus laughed.

"You wouldn't be the first to think that of him. Now then – you know you agreed it would be good for development people to see the country properly? What about putting your money where your mouth is and coming back to Brikaba with me when I go at the end of the week. See something of the place apart from defunct aid projects."

"That would be great. I've got a week's leave carried over from last year. We couldn't go tomorrow, could we? There's a dinner engagement I'd do almost anything to get out of."

"Alas, no. The Bishop has summoned me and his word must be obeyed. I'll see you at the bus park on Saturday morning. Six thirty."

"Bus park?"

"You said you wanted to see the country properly. What better way could there be?"

Brighton, June 15th 1996

POST CARD

Back in England – thought
I could do with a piano base
for the next few years. Sang
in concert at the Wigmore
Hall last week – reviews
weren't bad. You may have
seen the one in The Times –
isn't that what diplomats in
peaceful European cities do
all day? Read the papers?
Or go shopping for haute couture? R x

Daniel Maslolison
FCO Paris
c/o King Charles St.
London SW1A 2AH

B aboucar opened the door and grinned at Daniel. "Good evening, Mr Daniel. Come in."

"What are you doing here?" Daniel shook his hand warmly. "A spot of moonlighting?"

"Moonlight?" Baboucar peered past Daniel at the night sky.

"Don't worry. It's just a silly expression. Are you working for the Barlings this evening?"

Before Baboucar had the chance to reply, Jackie Barling swept up to Daniel and kissed the air beside his cheeks three times, a habit with which she had returned from her recent holiday in France. At least, thought Daniel, as she led him through to the drawing room, he would not have to spend the next five minutes in the loo scrubbing the scarlet imprint from his face.

"So glad you could come at such short notice, Daniel. I do so hate to have an odd number round the table. It looks so messy. We've invited Bob Newpin, too."

"Oh God."

"Sorry?"

"Oh good. What's Baboucar doing here?"

"I've taken him on as a waiter for the evening. It's so much easier entertaining when there's staff, don't you think? Right, everybody," Jackie called out gaily, betraying for a moment her nursery school teacher origins, "this is Daniel Maddison."

"Our new boy at the office," continued Len Barling, slapping him on the back and propelling him towards the guests. "Well, not so new now. How long's it been – six – seven months? Anyway, Daniel, this is Annette Jacobs, our colleague from the visa section in Dakar, Clare Evans from the British Council in good old London, and I think you know Bob Newpin."

"Damian! Good to see you, mate." Newpin hooked his arm through Daniel's and led him out to the veranda. "Exciting times, eh?"

"Are they?"

"Just about got the go-ahead."

"Go-ahead for what?"

"The timeshare complex. You know – up in Brikaba."

"I thought you were going to build on the coast?"

"Old hat, mate, old hat. I'm going for the ethnic theme – you know, drums in the African night, walks under the clear, starlit skies. The simple, yet luxurious. Ikea meets Hotel Intercontinental—"

"Baden-Powell meets Robert Powell?"

"Yer what?"

"Nothing. Have you ever been to Brikaba?"

"No, but ask me again in a week and the answer will be yes. I'm off up there at the weekend."

Daniel groaned.

"You all right, mate? Got a touch of the Bakinabe Belly? I tell you, Damian, I've been to the lav that many times, I feel like one of those baboon things – you know, the ones with the multi-coloured arses on them."

"Dinner's served, everyone," called Jackie, clapping her hands, her many rings chinking.

She placed Daniel between Clare Evans and Annette Jacobs and sat down opposite them, nestled between her husband and Bob Newpin.

Daniel tried his best. He chatted to Clare from the British Council who, though pleasant enough, looked about as uncomfortable as he felt and kept glancing surreptitiously at her watch. He attempted a conversation with the visa officer from Dakar but, having ascertained that he was neither a Hash House Harrier nor an Arsenal supporter, she clearly found him intolerably dull and turned her attentions to Bob Newpin.

Clare Evans made her excuses – she had a plane to catch early the next day – and left for her hotel, little realising that everyone present knew that the one flight a week to Heathrow left in the afternoon. With her, and most of the wine, gone the atmosphere became more relaxed.

"So what do you think of Fenella, then?"

Daniel looked up from his coffee and After Eights to see Jackie looking at him with an oddly arch expression.

"Erm – she's very nice."

"No. About her and that Finn. In Dakar."

"I'm afraid you've lost me there."

"Annette here saw them on Gorée," continued Len, relishing the situation. "Having a romantic dinner at that French hotel on the quay. Hours after the last ferry for the mainland had left, so they must have been staying together."

"No wonder she comes back from her bridge club at the Finnish Embassy looking like the cat that got the cream. I've a good mind to take up bridge myself. Only joking, Len darling."

"Does Alec know?" asked Daniel. "He was in a very odd mood the other day."

"I doubt it. Probably far too busy making up for lost time with Hélène Smets."

"Hélène Smets?"

"Daniel," said Len with genuine concern. "Do you

exist on the same planet as the rest of us? You must know about him and Mr Smets's lovely wife."

"No. I thought his tastes were—"

Daniel stopped. What on earth was he doing? First there was Patrick sounding like some old Tory and now he was sounding like something out of a *Sun* editorial. The world was going mad.

He had never imagined that he would be reprieved by a Len Barling home video, but now, as he sat gazing at the Barlings white-water rafting down a river in the Dordogne, he felt blessed. Then he felt something vibrating. Djin, the Barlings' shih-tzu, a direct descendant of Fenella's Mimi, was mounting his leg.

"Djin! You naughty little boy! Come here, Djin-Djins. Look – come here."

Jackie took an After Eight from its neat brown envelope and held it out to the dog. He sniffed it from a distance.

"Len, darling. Crack open another Baileys, can you?" As Jackie was looking over at her husband, the dog licked the chocolate that was still suspended at arm's length. It wrinkled its nose and wandered off. Jackie turned back to Daniel, lifting the chocolate to her lips as she did so. Daniel looked on, horrified.

"Is anything the matter?" she asked.

"No," he said, "I'm absolutely fine, but I really must be going now. It's getting very late. Thank you so much for a lovely evening."

As he got up to leave, Jackie popped the After Eight into her mouth and Daniel smiled for the first time that evening.

151

Thomas Kayne crouches over an enamel bowl of fish and rice, separating the flesh from the tiny bones with his fingers. A young boy in bright orange shorts moves away from the group of children who are eating by the fire and squats down beside him. He reaches into his pocket and takes out a tiny kitten. He holds it out to the old man. One of its eyes is missing, the other stares, wide-eyed, at the old man's food. The boy puts the kitten down and watches it stagger towards the visitor. Thomas Kayne reaches out to it, a piece of fish in his hand. The kitten pounces on the food, its coarse tongue grazing over the man's rough palm. *Faturu. Belado faturu.* Hungry cat. Hungry. He was too hungry for love. Scraps. Scraps of love are not enough. The child scoops the kitten up and places it on his shoulder. It clings on unsteadily, sniffing the child's ear.

Thomas Kayne finishes his meal, then gathers up his blanket and stick. He raises a hand in farewell and walks away back into the bush.

Daniel did not need to concentrate very hard to work out why his lap felt warm and wet. The sleeping baby that he had been handed in the crowded bus had woken up and was looking up at him with large, serious eyes. Daniel tried to turn his head to see if he could identify the baby's mother but found himself coming eye to eye with a disgruntled, scabby chicken in a wicker basket. He wondered how Father Seamus was doing, last seen crushed up against a melancholy European woman somewhere towards the back of the bus. The priest had looked extremely hot and uncomfortable, the young woman strangely serene.

Despite the cramped conditions, the hours had passed remarkably fast. Daniel had spent much of the journey asleep, waking only once or twice as the bus swerved round sleeping dogs and unmarked holes in the road, to find his nose buried in soft black hair. He hoped the baby's mother would not notice the trickle of saliva that ran down the back of its neck where Daniel had dribbled as he slept.

They arrived in Brikaba at dusk. A young boy raced up to Father Seamus who picked him up and swung him round, laughing.

"Feck me, Abdulai Jammeh. If you don't stop growing soon, it'll be you swinging me round, so it will."

"And Miss Susie! You are come back too!" The child shook her hand, grinning broadly.

Father Seamus's travelling companion delved into her rucksack and pulled out a semi-liquid bar of Cadbury's Fruit and Nut.

"You see? I kept my promise. Ask Sister Mary Philomena if you can stick it in her fridge for a bit. How's your family?"

"Very fine, thank you."

"Daniel – this is our good friend Abdulai Jammeh." The priest beamed down fondly at the boy. "You may be seeing more of him next year if he gets into the High School. You probably know the aunt who'll be looking after him. Isatou?"

"Isatou Jammeh? At our visa office? I didn't know she came from round here. She looks such a city girl. Well, that'll be great."

"And I don't think you've met Susie – there wasn't really enough oxygen in that bus to waste on introductions. Susie's a VSO volunteer who's teaching agricultural science up here. And a very good teacher she is too."

Daniel held out his hand, but she was already heaving her rucksack onto her back, her ears burning red from the priest's compliment.

"Will you come and have some supper with us, Susie?" asked Father Seamus.

"No thank you, Father, I'd better get back." She cast a not entirely friendly glance at Daniel. "You've got rather a full house and they'll be expecting me in the compound. Tell your mother I'll be in the garden tomorrow morning, Abdulai, could you?" She turned off the road and trudged listlessly into the bush.

By the time they reached the Mission, the damp patch on Daniel's crotch had dried, leaving an incriminating tide-mark and a slight smell of ammonia. Sister Mary Philomena was at the door to welcome them. She gave them all a hug and ushered them in. She had prepared a wonderful meal of chicken stew with rice and an extra bowl for Abdulai Jammeh to take to his family. The child left for home reluctantly, wielding a large torch and promising to be back in the morning with some okra from his mother's vegetable garden.

"Guess who I had staying here the other day?" asked Sister Mary Philomena as they sat down to eat.

"Now let me think. That nice Ghanaian priest from Kumasi?"

"I should be so lucky! No, you're on the wrong track completely."

"Oh, I don't know … the Imam of Kantaba?"

"No."

"Just give me a clue, can't you, woman?" Father Seamus laughed. "The Queen of Sheba."

"Closer. Rachel Kayne."

"Good God!"

"She's in Dakar," said Daniel. "There can't be three of them."

Sister Mary Philomena frowned. "Three Rachel Kaynes?"

Over the after-dinner drinks of whatever it was that Sister Mary Philomena made her famous alcohol out of, Daniel told them about the Rachel Kayne at Oxford, and they told him about the other Kayne, Thomas the wandering judge.

"She told me he was her grandfather," said Sister Mary Philomena. "But that's all. I tried asking her some questions about him but she wouldn't say any more. She's a strange one, that Rachel Kayne. She may not say anything with her voice, but her eyes say a lot."

"Do you think that's true?" asked Daniel.

"God, yes," said Father Seamus. "Don't you? There's a terrible sadness in them."

"No, I'm sorry, I meant, do you think it's true that Thomas Kayne really is her grandfather."

"He could be." Sister Mary Philomena re-filled their glasses with the cloudy liquid. "There have always been the rumours and stories – you know the kind of thing. That he once killed someone and that made him go mad; that he came from a wealthy family back in England who ostracised him for some reason; that he has children sprinkled throughout the Sahel, and a fortune hidden somewhere, but I don't know how true any of it is, sure I don't."

"And then the thing about the house-boy that Isabel mentioned," said Daniel.

"The reality is probably much more mundane than that," Father Seamus continued. "I've never heard of an English grandchild, but then there wouldn't be any reason why I should have. He's been wandering for as long as any of us here can remember. Come to think of it, I'm not sure whether even his being a judge is true or just something we've all learned to believe because someone once thought he might have been. Did I tell you I saw him recently, Mary Philomena? Way out by the river."

"You did. So would you think that Rachel is here because of her grandfather?"

"Sounds possible. But it doesn't explain what she's doing selling cloth in the city. And living with that Lebanese trader."

"Where did she go, after Brikaba?" asked Daniel.

"I got her a lift to Kamina with the Save the Children

Fund people."

"How far is that?"

"About fifty miles or so. Thinking of going?" asked Father Seamus. "Is the public bus fixed, Sister?"

"It is, so. That's the nearest we've come to a miracle in recent decades. It was the fan belt."

Sister Mary Philomena could see Father Seamus's eyes glazing over with exhaustion. "Now come on, you two, off to bed. You're fit for nothing, either of you."

Fenella opened her case and tipped the contents onto the bed. Each item of clothing reminded her of Paavo; the bra that he had removed so dextrously, the nightdress that he had gently slipped off her shoulders, the skirt up which his hand had deftly crept during dinner at the Dakar Hilton. She picked up a blouse – the one she had been wearing when they had made love in the lift – and inhaled his strong, musky scent. Then the little gold dress with the silver threads that she had worn that night on Gorée. There was a small rip in one seam. It was all very well wearing a skin-tight little number, but getting out of it in a hurry, when faced with an aroused Finn, was not the easiest of tasks, particularly not after a couple of bottles of decent Sancerre.

As she lifted her head, smiling to herself at the memories, she saw Alec standing in the doorway.

"My God, Alec! How long have you been standing there like a lemon?"

He walked up to the bed and kissed her on what would have been her lips, had she not turned her face away.

"Had a good trip, darling?"

"Wonderful."

"Improved your handicap?"

"My what?"

"You know – bridge."

"There's only one thing handicapped around here."

"Sorry?"

"If you mean did my technique improve, I think I can say it did. Very much so. Well, they say practice makes perfect."

"Your partner thought so too?"

Fenella blushed a deep scarlet. "Oh, no doubt at all about that. In fact we're thinking of entering the next tournament. In Abidjan."

"Good idea," said Alec. "The break's brought quite a colour to your face."

"What about you? Managed to survive without me?" She paused to light a cigarette. "Made any significant diplomatic decisions likely to affect the political stability of the region? Entertained any world-renowned visiting dignitaries?"

Alec had turned to the window and was gazing out at the sea, drumming his fingers against the glass.

"Do stop that," she snapped. "Mimi's not up the duff, is she?"

Alec froze. "What? Oh, no," he said, as he realised with relief what she was talking about. "Just fat I think."

"Christ! I only have to be gone five minutes and Kaddy's stuffing her with rice and palm oil instead of grilled chicken. She'll have to go."

"Just because she's got a bit fat? Isn't that a bit harsh?"

"Not the dog, you idiot. Kaddy." Fenella gathered up her clothes and threw them into the laundry basket. "Haven't you got work to do, Alec? Or at least pretend to do?"

Alec looked at Fenella and took a deep breath.

"I don't quite know how to say this."

"What? I'd like to finish unpacking in peace if that's OK with you."

"I've been having an affair."

There was a short pause during which Alec held his breath. To his surprise, Fenella lit another cigarette. Apart from a slight tremor in her hands, she seemed quite calm.

"I'm sorry," he continued.

"What? Sorry you've had the affair, or sorry you've told me."

"Neither of those, really. Sorry to have hurt you."

"God – have you been watching a load of second-rate videos while I've been away? Sorry to have hurt you. Who do you think you are? Bloody Brian O'Neal?"

"Ryan, don't you mean?"

"Pedantic to the bitter end. Brian. Ryan. It doesn't really matter, does it? Now can I please unpack without an audience."

"Is that it, then?"

"Well, what do you want me to do? Throw myself weeping at your feet? I don't suppose it's the first, is it? Why you feel the urge to get dramatic about it all of a sudden is beyond me. Now just bugger off, there's a good boy, and don't do it again."

Fenella sat down on the edge of the bed, emptied her make-up bag onto it and began sorting out her cosmetics. When she looked up, Alec was still standing in front of the window.

"It's not that simple, I'm afraid," he said at last. "She's pregnant."

Fenella laughed bitterly. "I can just see her in one of those Mothercare sacks. Or what about a pair of pink dungarees? So much for Belgian chic! So how much is it going to cost you?"

"Cost me?"

"Flight to Brussels, few days in a private clinic. I can't see Hélène Smets slumming it somehow. Christ! I always knew she was a tart but I never thought she was a stupid tart. And I always knew that you were an idiot, but never, not even in my wildest dreams, did I ever think you were that much of an idiot."

"It's not Hélène. I'm sorry."

"Stop bloody apologising. It's getting on my nerves." She paused for a moment. Alec braced himself. "What do you mean, it's not Hélène?"

"I've never had an affair with Hélène."

"Try telling that to anyone round here."

"I haven't. I'm sorry."

"If you say you're sorry again, I may well kill you."

Alec glanced at the nail scissors on the bed and took a step back.

"Who is it then?"

"Isatou."

Fenella stared at him as though he was mutating into an alien before her eyes, her features registering a mixture of shock, fury and disbelief.

"Serves the bloody Jungle Bunny right! Well," she spat, "at least terminations come cheap here. Some filthy witch doctor will probably do it for a packet of fags. Here – take these!" She flung the packet at Alec's head. Dunhills rained down around him.

"I'm sor—"

"Just shut the fuck up and get out. And don't come back until you've got rid of her and that stinking foetus."

"She's not getting rid of it."

"What do you mean?"

"I mean Isatou's going to have the baby."

"Make her get rid of it. Pay her."

"I couldn't possibly do that."

"You're going to have a baby with a black clerk?"

"She's not a clerk."

"Why?"

"Because she's an administrator."

"No, you imbecile. Why are you having the baby?"

"It's what we want to do."

It was the "we" that did it for Fenella. When she spoke again, it was with quiet, but venomous, incredulity.

"Let me get this right. You expect me to say that it's fine for you to have a baby with some local administrator, some fat, black local administrator? What do you plan to do? Move her into the spare bedroom? Dandle the bastard, frizzy-haired infant on your lap at dinner parties? Go on! What do you plan to do?"

"It's all come as a bit of a surprise, really. It's not a situation I ever imagined I'd be in. The children thing."

"We never wanted any."

"Any what?"

"Children, what do you think? Well? Did we?"

Fenella watched him condescendingly as he struggled to find the words with which to answer her. He opened his mouth to speak, but nothing came out. Then, as it gradually dawned on her what he might say if he were to find the words, she changed tack, her tone very slightly less abrasive.

"So what does your porky paramour think about it all?"

"Please, Fenella."

"Please what?"

"Please don't be like that – about her. If you want to be angry, and you've every reason to, be angry with me."

"Oh, don't worry, I will. I've barely begun. You still haven't answered my question."

"I don't know. It's all a bit of a mess. We just know that we love each other."

"Ah – sweeeeet! And what does that mean in practical terms? What are you going to do with her?"

This time there was no hesitation.

"Marry her. When we're divorced, of course."

The silence that followed was one that Alec would not forget. The blood drained from Fenella's face.

"Divorced?" she echoed very quietly.

Then to Alec's utter amazement she sank down from the bed and lay weeping at his feet.

Eleanor Cameron watches Stanley Shea as he sleeps. She will leave soon. She does not think that she will come back. Vera has gone home, but not before her curiosity had been satisfied.

"Stan – what was he like then – in Africa?" she had asked.

"He was a lovely man. Very handsome."

"Oh yes?" she had said, smiling archly.

"No, there was never anything like that. He was – I was engaged to his best friend."

"And there's me been calling you Miss all this time."

"I never married."

"Oh, I'm sorry. Did he die out there? Your fiancé?"

"I suppose he did. In a way."

Vera had looked at her expectantly.

"I'm sorry," she had replied eventually. "These aren't really things I talk about. Not now, after so long."

"Bound to bring up all sorts of things, though, coming here. What made you look him up after all these years?"

"I don't really know. It felt like time to tie up a few loose ends."

"I'm more a one to let sleeping dogs lie. Loose ends have a habit of getting tangled up, in my experience."

They do, thinks Eleanor, they do. She looks at Stanley's face, peaceful again now. It should be me who weeps, not you, she thinks. There will be no answers for me, no neat endings. At least you knew why Musa Mohammed had to leave you. And now you know he never stopped thinking of you. *I never married.* It sounds so simple now. But there was nothing simple about Tom, with his wild moods that swung from exhilaration to despair, with his mad enthusiasms – his fossils, his birdwatching, his fascinations for those Fulani women. *I never married.* Why should I have married? There was only ever Thomas Kayne. At least your pain shows, Stanley, she thinks, bitterly.

"What happened?" she asks the sleeping form beside her. "After he travelled back to England with you? After what everyone persisted in referring to as 'the accident'."

She remembers the kiss Tom had given her at the harbour. A gentle kiss, devoid of passion. I'm sorry, he had whispered. What for? she had asked. You weren't to blame.

"He didn't come back. Did you know that, Stanley? After he took you home. He didn't ever contact me again. There were rumours, of course – about a hasty marriage to a woman he'd known before he went out to West Africa. And a child. A son. I didn't believe them. Then, years later, the wilder tales of him or his doppelganger roaming the Sahel." She smiles a slight, sad smile. "Those, at least, I half believed."

I never married. How many times had she tossed that phrase out lightly, as the grief swirled throughout her body. No, there are no neat endings in real life, she thinks as she gets ready to leave. She will telephone her niece again and arrange to go and visit. Better to spend time with the living than the dead. She kisses Stanley Shea on the forehead and turns towards the door.

Despite the heat and the flies, and the faint stink of sewage, Fenella Moss was starting to feel a bit better. She had found her way into the fetid heart of this cesspit of a city on her own and here she was, sitting in something that approximated to a café. All right, so she had instructed the driver to drop her at the nearby ferry terminal and wait for her there, but still. Jackie Barling, for all her white-water rafting and scuba diving (someone her size really should know better than to stuff herself into a wetsuit), would never have done anything half so daring.

After a while, she became aware of a presence at her side. A little girl of about seven or eight was standing at her elbow, looking up at her expectantly.

"Piss off," said Fenella.

The girl stood her ground.

"Go on. Bugger off and do your begging somewhere else."

"I've come to take your order, madam."

"Oh." Fenella took off her Ray-Bans. "Shouldn't you be at school?"

"It's Saturday. What would you like to have?"

"A bloody great gin."

"Ice, lemon and tonic?"

"No. Cyanide. What do you think?"

Fenella noticed that a very tall, very black man who was taking another order had turned round and was standing with his pen poised above his pad, listening to the conversation. There was something about his expression that suggested it might be prudent to try an alternative tone of voice.

"Actually, I'll have a cup of tea. You do have tea in this place?"

"Earl Grey, English Breakfast, Lapsang Souchong, Ceylon or Keemun China tea? Or we have herbal infusions, too." The child screwed up her face as she visualised the store cupboard. "Strawberry and Loganberry Splash; Vanilla and Ginger Surprise and Camomile. And Mint."

"God! I wish I'd never asked. English Breakfast." Then seeing the man was still looking at her, "Please," she muttered. Actually, he wasn't bad-looking, if you liked that sort of thing. Which she didn't. She saw him mutter something into the ear of a customer who was seated with his back to her. There was a roar of laughter.

"Come on, Ibraima!" the man's voice rang out. "Here? I don't think so! I don't suppose they even know here exists." He pulled the waiter down towards him and continued in a loud whisper, "You know they have a strange medical condition? They do. Really. They start to decompose if they ever leave the compound or spend more than five minutes in the company of anyone not originating from the Home Counties." The man was now laughing so much that he began to choke. He took off his canvas hat and stuffed it into his mouth while Ibraima patted him on the back. At last he pulled himself together and looked round.

"Good God! Fenella!" he said, wiping the tears from his eyes with a piece of hat. "What on earth are you doing here? And what have you done to your face? It's decomp— not your usual look."

It was that ridiculous Redmond chap, the one who

fancied himself as a poet. Fenella rummaged in her handbag and took out her powder compact. For a moment she thought some strange street person was standing behind her, rudely peering over her shoulder. Then, with a start, she recognised the person with the swollen pink nose, and puffy red eyes surrounded by large black smudges of non-water-resistant mascara.

"Shit!" She snapped the compact shut, dropped it back into her bag and put her sunglasses on again.

"I think that's being a bit hard on yourself. You don't look that bad – just different … from usual, as I said. Do you mind if I join you?"

"Yes I do, actually."

Undeterred, Patrick picked up his glass of beer, walked over to Fenella's table and sat down opposite her.

"Your uncle had better watch out, Sukai, or you'll be taking the place over," he said as Ibraima's niece returned with the tea and arranged the pot, cup and saucer, strainer, milk and slice of lemon carefully on the table. "And I'd better watch my back too, with your English being so good now." The child grinned proudly.

"That's a bit abstemious," Patrick said to Fenella, nodding at the teapot.

"All right. I'll have a whisky. A double. Since you're offering."

"I wasn't aware that I was. Oh well. Sukai – a whisky please. A double. So, Fenella." He paused and looked at her quizzically. "How are you?"

"It's all right. Laugh away. Everyone else will be soon enough."

"I wasn't laughing actually. This is my concerned

look. It's the best I can do."

"In that case, don't bother."

"What about this then?" Patrick raised one eyebrow, and gave a slight smile. "It's my politely curious look."

"I expect you're just after another poem. I seem to have provided you with plenty of copy in the past."

"Chance would be a fine thing. I've not had much inspiration for days. Been rather out of sorts lately."

"Oh, what a shame. My heart bleeds for you. Well, perhaps just a limerick then." She fixed him with a bitter look. "There was an old woman who cried / 'My mascara has run down one side …' "

"That's not bad, actually," said Patrick. "Look – here's your whisky. And – er – have a hanky." He delved into his pocket, rummaged around unsuccessfully, then passed her his hat. Fenella snatched it from him and dabbed angrily at a sooty tear that was emerging from under her sunglasses. Then she lit a cigarette and dragged deeply.

"I may as well tell you." She exhaled. "It'll be round every bloody High Commission in the former colonies by the end of the week." She stared out over the river. "The bastard got the bitch pregnant."

"Which particular bastard got who pregnant?"

"The bastard Alec and some … some filthy black filing clerk or other. What's the tart's name … Isatou."

"Isatou!" Patrick roared.

"I know! If it was black flesh he was after, you'd think he could have gone a bit more upmarket – some ambassador's wife or something – there're plenty of them ready to spread their legs for anyone – not some office menial."

"Isatou!" Patrick repeated, horrified.

"I know! That was my reaction entirely."

"And I suppose he's just going to say it was all a bit of a mistake – a temporary aberration – take her down an alleyway somewhere behind the market. Pay some … some quack to get rid of the thing as quickly as possible and continue as before? Maybe pay Isatou a few lamasi to keep her mouth shut. Then sack her from her job. And let's say no more about it."

Fenella looked at Patrick with more warmth than she had ever before mustered in his presence.

"You'd think so, wouldn't you, Patrick? That's what anyone with an ounce of sense would do. But oh no. Not our Alec. They're going to have the tawny bastard. And what's more, the bastard won't even be a bastard. Good old Alec's only going to marry the slag."

"Alec's going to marry Isatou?" Patrick said faintly. "Why?"

"My words exactly. And you know what he said? Do – you – know – what – he – said? Well let me tell you. He said because we love each other."

Patrick put his head in his hands.

Fenella reached out and touched him. "At least you understand me, Patrick. I should never have thought so badly of you. Where are you going?"

Brighton, September 10th 1997

Well, so much for diplomats
having nothing to do in Paris.
Amazing how Diana's death
has moved the world.
It was the image of the
two boys walking behind he
coffin that was the worst.
I find, increasingly, that I can
no longer bear to watch the news.
R x

Daniel Madolisan
FCO Paris
c/o King Charles St
London SW1A 2AH

Daniel lay on his narrow bed in the cell-like guest room, listening to the quiet murmur of voices, punctuated by laughter, that floated through the thin wall. Sister Mary Philomena had been mortified to discover that the spare sheets had not been washed, and deeply apologetic that Daniel would have to sleep in used linen. But Daniel found it strangely erotic to be lying naked between sheets in which, only a few days before, Rachel had slept. He wondered if the material (candy-coloured striped cotton that had been the essence of chic in the early seventies) had come from H. A. Sharif and Sons, and whether Rachel, too, had lain naked and sweating in the still, humid air, watching the shadows play on the ceiling.

The voices in the adjoining room grew quieter. Daniel heard the creak of the armchairs. Father Seamus and Sister Mary Philomena must be getting ready to go to bed. He turned over to switch off the lamp. It was then that he caught sight of something wedged between the bed and the bedside table. He lowered his hand into the narrow gap and felt around. His fingers identified a thick spine and a hard cover. He manoeuvred the book out of the gap and held it close to the lamp. It was some kind of notebook. Daniel's heart began to beat faster as he flicked through the well-worn pages. A few pressed bougainvillaea petals fell onto the bed. He stopped at the last entry, and scanned the first few lines.

The hotel wasn't there any more, Tahir. Nothing else seemed to have changed much. The same noises, the same sound of children playing and the smell of cooking. I think I recognised the compound where that baby had just been born. She was so perfect – do you remember? Her mother was so proud. You picked her up and passed her to me. You put your arm around me and I nearly told you then. The Catholic Mission where I am staying tonight feels so safe. I could stay here forever – here in this tiny room. But I have to go on.

The entries – each separated from the one before by a line of tiny stars – were not dated but they appeared to go back for many months; or even years, it was hard to tell. Daniel knew that he should shut the notebook, that there was something deeply treacherous about what he was doing, but he could not stop reading. He opened pages at random, searching for evidence of some other kind of life – a life that included the ordinary, the mundane minutiae of everyday life – but there was none.

I think of you when he's inside me. He becomes you. It's the only way I can bear it. I know he knows what I am doing. I can see the disgust in his eyes. Disgust and desire, hatred and pity. But it suits us both. So we carry on. Each of us using the other.

I dreamt of you again last night, Tahir. The same dream I have so often. Your hands reached down to me as I drowned.

I should leave. But how can I now? If there is any chance – any hope – I should stay. For you. I get glimpses, sometimes, of another existence. It's like seeing a chink of light through the bars of a prison window. For a moment I think that I could just soar away up into the sky, but I'm like one of those caged birds that has forgotten how to fly. It sees the open door and just puts its head under its wing.

Daniel noticed that his hands were shaking. He felt as though he had ripped open a packet of love letters and left them scattered over the floor in a betrayal of crushed rose petals and torn ribbon. There was nothing to link the notebook to Rachel – no name or address on the front page – but it had to be hers. Part of him wanted to push it back into the narrow gap next to the bed and pretend that he had never found it, go back to the city and forget about it. But another part of him knew that he had to return it to Rachel, even though the thought of her knowing that he had read her notebook filled him with something approaching terror.

He thought back to Oxford and tried to remember who she was with then. Had there been a Tahir? Could it be that Rachel? But when he pictured her, surrounded by her beautiful, clever friends, everyone else was a blur – it was her face alone that he could see, laughing. Then Daniel remembered something. She had disappeared. Sometime during their final year, she had simply ceased to be there. The beautiful, clever people were all still about, clutching their bottles of champagne or Pimms as they strolled from party to party, from theatre to concert hall, but they were no longer orbiting around the sun that had been Rachel.

He never could bring himself to penetrate the force field of privilege, confidence and talent that surrounded Rachel's crowd, and ask someone who might have known what had happened to her. What would he have asked them? He had never even spoken to her.

He picked up the notebook again. It fell open on the last page. He saw that the last lines written were the words of a poem. *Had I the heavens' embroidered cloths*, it began. Daniel frowned. There was something so familiar about those words. Then he remembered. So there was, finally, something to link the two Rachel Kaynes.

Daniel put the notebook on the bedside table and turned off the light. He lay in the dark, thinking. From next door, there was a muffled giggle, another creak of an armchair. His eyes began to close. It was just as he was going to sleep that he had a sudden, and very clear, revelation. The room next door was not the Mission's sitting room. It was Sister Mary Philomena's bedroom.

"Rachel?"

Kamal walked out onto the veranda and called again. "Rachel? I'm back."

His voice bounced back off the high wall that surrounded the garden. He heard the tired rattle of the watchdog's chain. The frangipani blossom glowed in the moonlight, its sweet scent reminding him of the young Chinese cloth merchant, her pale, smooth skin pulled taut over her high cheekbones, her tiny hands caressing the samples as she held them up for him. Later, she had caressed him too, his body melting into satin under her gentle touch. He shook the memory from his mind.

"Rachel?" His voice was angry now.

He heard footsteps behind him.

"About time," he said tersely, keeping his back to the door.

Faysal looked at his watch as he walked over to Kamal and embraced him.

"Am I late for something? I didn't know you were expecting me. I just called in to see how the trip went. Welcome back."

He sat down and lit a cigarette with a heavy gold lighter. "Sorry!" He held the packet out to his brother. "Try one. American. New range. They're selling well."

"No. Thanks."

"Are you all right?"

"Of course, why not? And you and Suhad?"

"Fine, both fine."

"And how was Dakar?"

"Dakar was as beautiful as ever. I tell you, Suhad's

cousin's new house is a palace. And the yacht! I suppose that's what you get if you trade in diamonds rather than cigarettes and cars."

"Or cloth."

"You can't complain," Faysal laughed, gesturing at the house and garden.

"And Rachel," Kamal continued. "Did she enjoy it?"

"Rachel?"

"My 'wife'," he replied, with heavy irony.

"Yes – I know who you mean. But what about her?"

"Look, Faysal. I've had a very long day. I've come home to an empty house. I don't even know what time zone I'm in. You took her to Dakar with you, remember?"

"No."

"What do you mean, no?"

"She didn't come. We were having dinner here when she said she'd rather stay at home."

"Well, where did she go then? When I rang from Shanghai, the maid said she'd gone to Dakar with you and Suhad. And put Yussuf in to cover the shop."

"We haven't seen her since that evening."

Kamal leant towards the table and picked up the packet of cigarettes. He took one out and rolled it between his finger and thumb. Faysal blew a smoke ring which floated up towards the ceiling then out into the garden where it dissolved into the warm night. After a while, Kamal picked up the lighter and lit his cigarette. They sat smoking, listening to the night.

"She'll be back," Kamal said at last.

Faysal looked up. "Sorry?"

"Rachel. She'll be back." Faysal said nothing. "Well?" Kamal asked angrily.

"Well what?"

"You disapprove. You always have done."

"You're hardly one to let other people's disapproval affect you. You wouldn't have all this if you did."

"You know what I mean."

"Look, Kamal. What you do with your life is your business. "

"She'll be back."

"See – whether or not I approve is neither here nor there as far as you're concerned, and that's fine by me. It's late and I'm going home. I hope you're right," he added as he gathered up his lighter and cigarettes. "Oh, by the way, that little property developer has been asking for you. He tracked me down to the warehouse last week and demanded to know when you'd be back. Said he had a proposition for you."

"Oh yes?"

"Something about Brikaba Camp – what was it he said? The Ultimate Bush Experience. But then he made some lewd joke about it, based on the many uses of the word bush, and I rather lost the thread."

"The man's a peasant. Perhaps you should have pointed out to him that if I'd wanted to build a hotel in the bush, I'd have done it by now and without the help of a second rate little 'tycoon'."

"So how come he thinks you're going to go into business with him?"

"I really couldn't tell you. Tunde N'Jie introduced us when I last went over to the Ministry – months ago. But I didn't expect to hear from him again."

"I wouldn't put money on it that you won't. He's a persistent little fellow."

"That's one way of describing him. But when we met he was talking about developing down here, on the coast, not up-country on the river. He must be mad if he thinks I'd put money into a scheme like that."

"He must think there's a good chance you will. He's up there in Brikaba now."

"Well, let's hope he stays there. Look – have a drink."

"Thanks, but I ought to be getting back. Suhad's very tired these days. She's getting pretty big."

There was a brief silence.

"How's it going?" Kamal asked.

"Fine. Thanks. Look, I know it's difficult for you."

"What makes you think that?"

Kamal's eyes were frosty, daring his brother to expand.

"Nothing. Look, I must get back. I'll call by tomorrow."

Kamal shut the front door behind him, switched on the fan and sat down at his desk. His temples were throbbing. He sat with his head in his hands for a few moments, before taking a key from his wallet and opening the top drawer. With both hands he drew out a large leather binder and placed it on the desk. He stroked the smooth, warm cover, then opened it. To each page was stapled a small piece of material, beginning with the rough indigo cloth of the north, and the crisp Egyptian cotton that his grandfather had traded in. Then there were the damasks, the organdies and satins, the Dutch tie-dyes; then new synthetics of the fifties and sixties, the multi-coloured polyesters, the dralons, crimplenes, the nylons and the acrylics. He bent towards his open briefcase, brought out a handful of samples and laid them out in front of him. The desk sprang to life in an iridescence of Chinese silk – aquamarine, saffron, carmine and cerulean. He ran his fingers through them, brushed them against his lips, smelt their newness. His fingers wavered between the squares. No, not the aquamarine – too much like Rachel's eyes – clear, cold and challenging. The carmine. He would choose that in memory of the fire that had ignited inside him as the Chinese girl had run her hands over his naked body. With a decisive click, the silk square brought the history of the business, and Kamal's life, up to date.

There was something deeply satisfying about the feeling of warm sweat making its hesitant way between your breasts, trickling slowly over your stomach, brimming over your navel, then dripping confidently down your legs to the ground, thought Susie, as she leant against the bar in the tiny roadside liquor store. Something vaguely erotic, even, and a lot more satisfying than the odd fumble with Neil.

It was amazing, she mused, how the prolonged absence of any physical contact, with little hope of a reprieve, could bring together two people who found each other so completely unattractive in every sense. The fact that they were both volunteers, and both lonely – though Neil was far too macho to admit that – was the only thing they had in common. Still, at least mid-grope with Neil she could disappear into her favourite fantasy; Father Seamus would gaze into her eyes, suddenly overcome by an uncontrollable passion for her, immediately renounce his faith and whisk her off to an isolated croft in Ireland where they would make fervent love in front of a roaring peat fire. Occasionally her agricultural training got the better of her and she would try substituting a greener form of fuel, but the alternative was never as satisfying.

The bar was known to the entire volunteer community as the Last Chance Saloon. You had to be pretty desperate to spend an evening in the murky, cramped confines of what was essentially a roadside shack with a sticky wooden counter and a couple of rickety bar stools. The beer was always warm and the barman – Uncle Peacock – always drunk. This evening, as most, he was snoring loudly, his head resting on the counter. Susie finished off her beer and grimaced. She wished, now, that she had stayed in her compound. She would have eaten her bowl of rice and vegetables prepared by the senior wife, chatted for a while to the teenage daughters, watched the scrawny kittens nimbly stalking cockroaches, then spent the rest of the evening lying on her bed in the sweltering heat, listening to the World Service.

Abdulai Jammeh might have turned up to keep her company, leafing through her photograph albums. There was little he did not know about her family by now. But now that she was here she may as well have another drink.

She walked round the counter, avoiding Uncle Peacock's sleeping form, and opened the dormant fridge.

"Well, fuck and bugger it!"

Susie turned round to see a stocky white man, with thin, damp hair plastered over his bullet-shaped head.

"Not quite the barmaid I was expecting! Still, who's complaining. Not me! Relief to see a white face. I'll have a beer and have one yourself."

"I'm not the barmaid," said Susie in her usual expressionless voice. She nodded in the direction of the snores. "But thanks, anyway." She picked out a couple of bottles and put them on the counter.

"D'you come here often?" Newpin enquired, his eyes roving over her batik shift.

"That's ten lamasi altogether," said Susie, giving him a withering glance that passed him by. She took his money and left it on the shelf.

"Christ, that's a bloody bargain! I paid nearly ten times that the other week." He took a half-empty bottle from his jacket pocket and held it out. "Whisky chaser?"

Susie shook her head. Newpin took a swig from the bottle.

"So what's a pretty young thing like you doing in a town like this?"

"I live here."

"What? Here?"

"Well, not in this particular bar, obviously. In the next village."

"Christ! Your company must pay you well, to be stuck way out in this shit-hole. Makes Jeddah seem like fucking Rio de Janeiro, and they pay enough there, I can tell you. Made my first million there."

"Million what?" Susie asked, her voice resonating boredom.

"Well, rials. But that's still quite a lot, you know."

"Good for you."

"Thanks! I was pretty pleased with myself and all. Sorry! Never introduced myself. Bob Newpin. Managing Director of New Pin Enterprises. 'Timeshares for those with times to share.' And you are?"

"Susie Ashton. And no they don't pay me a lot – hardly anything actually. I'm not exactly here for the money."

"What are you here for then?"

"I don't know. The experience, I suppose."

"You can stay in England for that, I reckon. All you have to do is eat a packet of past-their-sell-by-date prawns, turn the heating up to max, put on some Bob Marley and spend a few days throwing your guts up in the bog."

"It's not quite the same."

"I think you'll find it is, love. Just bring in a few blacks and there's plenty of those around. Ever been to Brixton? You'd be lucky to see a single white face there these days."

Susie stared at Bob Newpin, wondering if he could possibly be being ironic.

"Well, what are you here for then? Were they out of prawns at your local Tesco's?" she asked, draining her beer and getting ready to leave.

"Come again? Oh, I see. Very funny. No. I'm here to make my second million. But this time, it'll definitely be in pounds sterling."

Susie laughed. "What are you going to do? Develop a timeshare complex in Brikaba?"

"Got it in one."

"You are joking?"

"Never more serious. It'll be bloody brilliant. I'll be building smack bang in the middle of yer 'real Africa'."

"And what good's that going to do anyone here? In this particular bit of 'real Africa'? Where one in four babies die before they're five. The malaria's chloroquine resistant, you know. Life's precarious enough up here. All it takes is just one swarm of locusts to bring the people to their knees. You'd do better to invest in the community."

Bob Newpin gazed at Susie as though she were a harmless, but ultimately deranged, creature from another planet. So what if she sounded like the 'facts in brief' section of the *New Internationalist*, she thought. She was not going to let Newpin get away with it so easily. Her face became animated; her voice rose above its usual monotone. "Look, I've been working on a women's garden project. It's really getting off the ground. With a bit more money, we could set up vegetable gardens all through the region. OK, so you wouldn't get much back beyond your original loan, but think of the satisfaction you'd get."

"I'm not quite sure you get it, sweetie. New Pin Enterprises isn't in the business of hand-outs. Plenty of do-gooders out here to do all that. And anyway, I've always been of the opinion that charity begins at home. The Lions Club's my thing. We bought a minibus for the little spastic kiddies just the other year."

"But what would you do for water? And electricity? And staff? And what would you do with all the waste? And what about the traffic?"

"What is this? Bloody *Mastermind*?" Newpin took a large swig from his whisky bottle. "Where there's a will there's a way, I always say. And where there's not a will or a way, there's always the old backhander to oil the wheels of commercial enterprise. I reckon one of the big shots in town – Arab guy, what is he? Lebanese, that's it – I reckon he'll come in with me and they say he's one of the richest men in the country. And the toffs at the Embassy are eating out of my hand."

"You haven't answered my question."

"What question?"

"The water and electricity and stuff."

"We'll bring in a bloody great generator. And sink a bloody big borehole." Newpin's speech was becoming indistinct. "And dig a bloody great pit for the rubbish. And honk to get the goats and kids off the roads. Goats and kids, geddit? Eh? Geddit? That OK for you, sweetheart?"

"No it's not. And don't call me sweetheart. What do you think the borehole will do to the water table? Some of the wells run dry as it is."

"Keep your hair on," Newpin slurred, picking up a strand of Susie's light brown hair and twisting it round his fingers.

She pulled her head away. "And how are you going to staff the place? I suppose you'll stick in some expatriate manager and give all the shit jobs to villagers for peanuts and forget to tell them that it's seasonal. And they'll leave their vegetable gardens to rot and then it'll be too late."

"I love it when a girl gets really angry. Shows a bit of spirit. Come here."

Newpin pulled Susie towards him. His bottle of beer fell over and flooded the counter.

"Get off me," she shouted.

"You must be gagging for it. Up here in the middle of nowhere. It's probably been months since you've had any."

"You're hurting my arm."

Newpin crushed her against the wall and yanked up her dress. "Relax, you silly cow. You'll love it. They all do. They just pretend they don't, in case I think they're easy."

Susie twisted her head round and sank her teeth into Newpin's cheek. He let out a furious yell and clutched at his face. "You bloody bitch!" he shouted.

Uncle Peacock raised his head from the beer-sodden counter, and stared blearily at Newpin. "Can I help you, mister?"

"She's the one who needs help – the stupid slag," Newpin spat as he turned to leave.

Susie's legs gave way beneath her, and she sank down to the floor, breathing heavily. Through the whooshing in her head, she heard the crunch of gears and the squeal of brakes as Newpin roared off into the sweltering night.

Daniel woke at dawn and lay listening to the sound of birds that he knew he should be able to identify by now. He had dutifully bought the *Field Guide to the Birds of West Africa* as soon as his posting had been confirmed. He had even been on a couple of organised birdwatching walks through the verdant acres of the scientific research institution opposite the High Commission. But though the act of spotting birds, ticking them off in the book and comparing notes with fellow twitchers carried with it a respectability, even a degree of machismo, that his brief juvenile interest in collecting train numbers had never done, he still found the whole thing faintly ridiculous.

The giggling sound of one of those green and yellow parrot-things reminded Daniel, with a jolt, of the sounds he had heard from the next room as he had drifted off to sleep. The house was silent. If he got up now, he would avoid the embarrassment of seeing them both come out of the same bedroom. He got dressed and walked out onto the veranda.

"Ah, Daniel! Come on and join us." Father Seamus closed the large black Bible on his lap. "It's the best time of the day, so it is. The only time to think. Before it gets too hot to do anything other than sweat like a pig. It'll be a blessed relief when the rains come, that's for sure."

"Coffee, Daniel my dear?" asked Sister Mary Philomena, putting down her sewing and picking up the coffee-pot.

"Thanks. That'd be lovely. But I don't want to disturb you. I thought I was the only one up."

"Away with you!" Father Seamus smiled. "You're

never disturbing us."

Sister Mary Philomena passed him a cup of coffee. "So, Daniel," she said, her eyes twinkling. "Let me guess, now. You'll be going to Kamina today?"

Daniel felt himself blush.

"Don't tease the poor boy, Sister!"

"Who's teasing, Father? I was just asking him if he was going to Kamina and where's the harm in that?"

"I don't want you to think I don't want to spend time here with you," Daniel said apologetically. "That was why I came, you know, not to trail after—"

"Nonsense, boy! Of course you must go," said Father Seamus. "There'll be plenty of other chances to spend time with us here. The good sister and I are unlikely to stray very far. I think if I was going to get a summons from His Holiness at the Vatican, it probably would have come by now. We'll be here for years, God willing, but who knows how long Rachel will be in Kamina? And, anyway, you've got the two of us wondering now. If you didn't go, we'd have something to say about it. And if you don't go now, before the rains, you'll be lucky to get there at all."

Daniel checked in at the Kamina government rest house a few hundred yards from the bus station. The manager handed him a key, a packet of candles and a box of matches. Then he winked at him. Daniel looked up at the numbered row of hooks behind the desk, and noticed that all the keys were there except for the one for room four. He looked at his key fob. Number three.

The room was bare but for a low wooden bed and a wardrobe. Leading off from it was a small bathroom.

Daniel stripped out of his grimy clothes and turned on the tap. It was then that he realised why there was a large plastic bucket filled with water. As he sluiced cold water over his body with the small measuring jug that had been hooked over the edge of the bucket, he began to feel rather foolish. He had had no plans beyond coming to Kamina to find Rachel. Now that he was here, he realised that he did not have a clue what he should do next.

By the time he was dressed, it was dark outside. He picked up the candles and matches and walked from his room onto the veranda that ran the length of the back of the building. He sat down on a low wooden chair, pausing to look up at the stars that filled the sky before lighting a match, dripping wax onto the table and sinking the base of one of the candles into it.

And that was when he saw her. She had been reading. It was too dark, now, to see the pages, but still she sat outside her room, a few feet from Daniel, the book in her hands. Daniel's mouth went dry. Rachel turned to look at him. Her face was pale and expressionless in the candlelight, her disembodied voice low.

"Why are you following me?"

"Sorry?"

"All that cloth-buying. And now this."

"What?"

"This. Are you going to tell me that both of us turning up in Kamina is some kind of amazing coincidence? Or maybe you had a sudden urge for a particularly exotic shade of chiffon and just had to find me to place an order?"

"No. Well, actually I didn't think you were here – until yesterday that is. I thought you were in Dakar.

I was staying at the Mission. On holiday. Sister Mary Philomena told me you were on your way here."

"So what do you want?"

"Nothing. I don't know."

"You know this would be called stalking back home. But I suppose you think it's all right here. I suppose the same rules don't apply when you're an expatriate." Rachel's voice, still low, brimmed with fury. "What do you think I am? Some mild diversion from your invaluable job of replicating completely useless aid projects? 'Oh look! There's someone who doesn't fit in. Let's follow her around and find out all about her.' You think it's OK to turn someone's life into an interesting story to amuse people with, to while away all those interminably dull evenings between drinks parties."

"You're not just a story."

What peculiar process went on in his brain, he wondered, between the formulation of a thought and its utterance? When he used to compose, back at Oxford, the cantata in his head had never come out as a Lloyd Webber musical on the page.

"Or does it offend your pathetic English sense of fair play that I appear to be living with a Lebanese? One of those filthy rich, uneducated, untrustworthy traders. 'So, new money.' Or selling cloth? 'Such a waste. And with her looks.' What about you? Living your absurd little life behind high walls in a country you know nothing about, hiding your ordinariness, your nothingness, behind your so-called status."

The candle flickered, sputtered and went out. Daniel picked up the matchbox. His hand was shaking. He put the matches down without lighting another candle. They sat in silence. In the distance, flashes of lightning lit up the humid night sky.

"I think I've met you before." His words floated out into the darkness.

"I know."

"No, before that."

"There is no before that."

"At Oxford."

Rachel said nothing.

"I remember you from Oxford."

Still Rachel remained silent.

Daniel took a deep breath. "I found your notebook at the Mission."

Rachel's voice, when she found it, was full of rage. "And you read it? So you don't just trail me around the city, follow me hundreds of miles and lie about recognising me. So tell me – explain your sick obsession."

"I'm sorry. I know it was wrong. I just wanted to find out if you were the Rachel Kayne I remembered from Oxford."

"So that makes it all OK, does it? You attempt to satisfy your pitiful curiosity by reading something that is quite obviously private. You're a ridiculous little creep. A ridiculous, obsessive little creep."

"Look, I've said I'm sorry. I've brought your notebook back. Here. You'd dropped it beside the bed at the Mission." He held it out into the darkness. "But if I'm obsessive, I'm hardly unique around here."

The notebook was snatched away. "Meaning what, exactly?"

"Nothing. I'm sorry."

"Go on! Tell me."

"No. I'm sorry I said it."

"No! Go on. You've read my notebook. Tell me."

"Well – all that stuff you wrote – to that man. That sounded pretty obsessive to me."

"You don't know anything."

"I know who you are – or were."

"You know nothing."

"I know who you are," Daniel insisted.

"You know nothing."

"It was the Yeats."

"What?"

Daniel hesitated. If he got this wrong, he knew that he would lose her. He struggled to find the right words. He took a deep breath. His clear tenor voice soared out into the darkness.

"Had I the heavens' embroidered cloths,
Enwrought with golden and silver light,
The blue and the dim and the dark cloths
Of night and light and the half-light ... "

When he stopped singing, Rachel's silhouette had changed shape. Her knees were drawn up to her chin, her arms encircled her legs. Neither of them spoke. Minutes, or maybe hours, passed. It seemed to Daniel as though he and Rachel were the sole inhabitants of some deserted, warm, black world, utterly alone, except for the cicadas which continued their song long after Daniel's had ended. When she finally spoke, it was with an air of quiet resignation.

"How do you know that arrangement?"

"I wrote it. I mean, I set the poem to music. At

Oxford. You sang it at its first performance. In the chapel at New College. Guido Ansaldi was there from Rome – on the lookout for new talent, they all said. You were wearing the most amazing purple dress. You looked like – like some kind of – I don't know. Some kind of purple angel."

There was a bitter laugh.

"Ethereal. That's how they described your voice in the reviews. I should really have hated you then. I don't think anyone remembered the song – just the voice."

"I did."

"I'm glad. I went up to congratulate you afterwards, but I couldn't get anywhere near. And then you disappeared. And when I next saw you it was in Tiokunda – at the market, then in the shop. I knew it couldn't really be you. That Rachel would have been in Milan or Rome or Vienna or somewhere. Dressed in purple and singing to adoring crowds. But I couldn't get you out of my head. Then I found out your surname and I thought there couldn't be two of you. But it was only when I read the poem in your notebook that I knew for sure who you were."

"You don't know who I am."

Daniel was silent. It was true. He knew no more about her now than he did when he first saw her in the market. And no more about her then than he had when she was at Oxford.

When Rachel next spoke, her anger seemed to have gone. He noticed an unfamiliar curiosity in her voice.

"I thought that 'The Cloths of Heaven' – the music for it – was written by two music undergraduates."

"It was."

"So what happened to the other one?"

"Jonathan Rosen." Daniel swallowed. "He's still writing music."

"You two were lovers, weren't you?"

Daniel felt the blood rush to his head. He did not reply.

"Now you see what it's like to have people make assumptions about your life, even if they turn out to be true," Rachel continued. "But at least I didn't have to read your diary to pass on that bit of information." There was a lighter, almost teasing, note in her voice. "It's crazy. I can hardly remember anything else about that time. I would never have recognised you, or even your name. But I remember what everyone said about the two of you."

"What?"

"That you must have composed that music in bed, it was so sensuous. Did you?"

"Did I what?"

"Write it in bed with Jonathan?"

"Of course I didn't."

"So now you're getting angry. And I've not even begun my obsession with you."

"It's not funny."

Rachel's voice turned serious again. "I wasn't being funny. I've long forgotten 'funny'."

"I'm sorry. We wrote it at a piano, actually. Over cups of tea."

"I wasn't really asking where you wrote it. I suppose I was asking if you loved him."

Daniel was silent.

"Love seems to have made you about as happy as it

has me," she said.

He could hear a rueful smile in her voice. He wished he could see her face, see what it looked like when not suffused with unhappiness or anger.

"So what happened – to the two of you? Come on – tell me about him. It can be your penance – for obsessive stalking in the face of considerable resistance."

What could he tell her about Jonathan? About his passion for Vivaldi, and obscure American detective novels, his laugh – the way his whole face creased up – the way he'd hold Daniel's head in his hands, the way he was always late for everything, his optimism? The evenings in tiny Soho bars; the weekend they spent in Barcelona; the day he'd met, and charmed, Daniel's parents; the time they went to the races with great-aunt Eleanor; those last few, terrible days before Daniel had left for Africa.

"He was my best friend."

"Just friends?"

"No." Daniel hesitated. "More than friends. Much more."

"So why all the secrecy? And why do you pretend he never existed?"

Daniel felt an intense sadness welling up inside him. His throat constricted.

"Jonathan wanted to compose. And I wanted a career in the Foreign Office."

"So?"

"It wouldn't have worked."

"What? He just couldn't come up with a way of sneaking a bit of manuscript paper and an HB pencil into the diplomatic bag? I can see it would've been a bit of a problem if he'd wanted to breed polo ponies. Or set up in private practice as a psychotherapist or specialise in neurosurgery."

"It wasn't that – he wanted to come."

"My God!" Rachel said, as she grasped the truth. "It was because of your job! It ended because you thought being 'out' would interfere with your meteoric rise through the ranks of the diplomatic service! You chose a career over someone you loved. And who loved you. And you think what I've chosen to do with my life is strange!"

Daniel shut his eyes for a moment. "It's too late now."

"Why?"

"It just is. Believe me."

"Well, I hope you think it was all worth it. For your marvellous diplomatic career."

"What gives you the right to sneer at the mess I've made of my life?" said Daniel, deeply hurt. "Yours doesn't exactly look too brilliant from where I'm standing. Living with someone you hate. Pinning all your hopes on tracking down some lover you haven't seen for years. I mean, for all you know, he could be dead."

"I do know."

"What?"

"That he's dead. I was with him when he died."

"My God. I'm sorry."

"Why should you be?" Rachel's voice cracked. "You never knew him."

Daniel wanted to put his hand out and touch her. "I thought, from what you'd written, that you were coming here to meet him."

"Maybe I was."

"Who is – was – he?"

"I suppose you've earned the story." Rachel paused. Through the darkness came the soft kuh-cooo of a white-faced owl. Daniel waited.

"He was called Tahir. I met him in the final term of my second year. He had rooms above mine. He was Lebanese – on a visiting fellowship from an African research institution. There was something about his energy. He was interested in everything – not just malaria – he was an expert on that – but music and art and books and people. I fell in love with him. Before I met him I'd felt like some reluctant queen bee or something. All those Oxford drones constantly circling me."

"I remember," said Daniel, his pain subsiding as her words floated out into the darkness.

"But loving Tahir – it was like some kind of incurable disease. My body ached when I wasn't with him. By the end of that term – when you saw me sing at New College – I had decided I had to be with him. I'd stopped caring about anything else – my degree, my singing – everything."

"So what happened?"

"My parents came up to Oxford for the concert. They took me out for dinner at the Manoir aux Quat' Saisons. Only the best for my father. I told them then that I was going to Bakinabe. They didn't react much. My father raised an eyebrow. My mother said it was an unusual place for a summer holiday. And then I told them about Tahir. Well, actually, I never did. I started telling them that I'd fallen in love with a man from Bakinabe and that I was going to go and live with him there. And then my father went completely mad."

"About you dropping out of Oxford."

"No. I'm not sure he was ever really convinced that an education did girls much good. He had always made it very clear what he thought of me reading Oriental Studies. It wasn't that. He said he'd known that the rotten genes would emerge somewhere, but that he'd never thought they'd surface in me. Another life thrown away in West Africa, he shouted. Another family torn apart by someone else's selfish love. The waiters looked nervous. My mother tried to calm him down, said she was sure it wasn't like that, but he wouldn't listen to her. What was it about Kaynes and black skin, he screamed. Everyone was looking at us."

"You said that Tahir was Lebanese."

"He was. But my father didn't stop long enough for me to tell him that. And it wouldn't have made any difference, probably. And anyway, I was so shocked by what he was saying that I just sat there. Then – and this was really strange – he stared straight at me and said weren't there enough black bastards out there without me adding another one."

Daniel tried to make sense of what she had just told him, wanted to ask her what she meant, but she carried on.

"And that was the last time I saw him. I can't remember anything else about that evening, apart from going to Tahir's rooms to tell him that I was going to Bakinabe with him as soon as his work at Oxford was finished."

"Was he pleased?"

"Surprised." Rachel laughed. "I think he'd assumed, like everyone else, that I'd finish my degree and go on to study singing in Europe. I'm not sure he ever thought our relationship would last beyond Oxford. But I didn't care. I just wanted to be with him, whatever that meant. If you'd met him, you'd have understood.

"The day before the end of term, my mother came to say goodbye. She'd had to come without telling my father where she was going. She looked awful. She said that, while she couldn't excuse the things my father had said that dreadful evening, she thought I might forgive him a little if I knew why he'd said them."

"Because he was a racist bigot?"

"That's rather what I suggested. No. She said that it was because of my grandfather. I thought she'd gone mad as well. I didn't have a grandfather. Her father had died about ten years before and I'd always known that my father had been brought up by his mother after his father had died."

"So who was he?"

"She didn't know much. Apparently my father's father had been in the Colonial Service in Nigeria. Then something happened out there – no one was ever sure what – and he left and came back to England. 'A broken man', they said. People speculated that it had been a disastrous love affair – most likely with a local girl. Shortly after that, he met my grandmother again – their families had always known each other – and they got married. They had a son very quickly. Then my grandfather became more and more unhappy and his behaviour more and more erratic, and when my father was about five, he disappeared.

"For a few moments I actually felt sorry for my father. His mother hired detectives to find her husband. It took several months, and then they traced him to West Africa – not to Nigeria, though, but to Bakinabe where he had, according to the detectives, 'gone bush'. After that, my grandmother must have decided it would be less of a humiliation to tell the world that he'd died."

"So when you told him you'd fallen in love with someone and were going to live in West Africa, he must have thought that history was repeating itself?"

"I suppose so. Anyway, I did go back with Tahir. There seemed to be even more reason to go then."

"To find Thomas Kayne?"

"Christ! Daniel!"

"I found out his name by accident. While trying to work out if you were – well, you know all that."

They sat in silence for a while. The lightning was getting stronger. They could hear the dull rumbling of distant thunder.

"So is that what you're doing here? Trying to find Thomas Kayne?"

"Yes. And no. I came here with Tahir. He loved the idea of the hunt for a long lost relative. He thought family was very important. He was never really happy that I'd had to choose between my family and him. We spent the first night in Brikaba then carried on to Kamina. We – we stayed here. We were sitting out on this veranda when I told him I was pregnant. I'd kept it quiet until then. I knew that he didn't love me as I loved him, and I wasn't sure how he'd react. But he was – I don't know – ecstatic. Once he knew I was carrying his child, our relationship became much, much more intense. We stayed here about a fortnight. I'd never been so happy."

Her voice, when she spoke again, was filled with a weary grief.

"One day, we went to one of the outlying villages where we'd heard a rumour that Thomas Kayne had been seen. We spent the day there, following up various leads. I told Tahir we shouldn't drive back in the dark – but he just kissed me and set off.

"I don't know what happened. When I came to, the car was lying on its side and Tahir wasn't there. He didn't believe in wearing seat belts. You don't need them if you're invincible. I found him lying a few yards away. He died in my arms. And as I lay beside him, I felt a terrible pain and our child bled away into the dust."

Thomas Kayne moves slowly through the bush. Now his bare feet feel sharp laterite where before they knew only dry grass. He sees the road stretching away into the distance, mottled brown and white in the moonlight. He peers through the darkness. The road to hell, the road to ruin. You'll go to hell, you know. Stop the frogs, stop the clocks. He looks up into the sky, at the stars now filtered through thin cloud. He is nearing the village. He can smell smoke, hear dogs barking.

Now he hears the sound of an engine far away. Going too fast, far too fast. You're a fast one, you are. He hears the screech of brakes and a dull thud. Then a voice – harsh – shocked – angry. Fukanbuggrit. Fukanbuggrit. Again the sound of an engine. Nearer now. Thomas Kayne is bathed in light and dust and then it is silent again. He walks on towards the village. Then he stumbles. At his feet is an orange and blue bundle. Fukanbuggrit. Fukanbuggrit. The words skip round in his head. Fukanbuggrit. Fukanbuggrit. Very slowly, he kneels down and touches the warm body of a small child. Thomas Kayne puts a gnarled hand onto the child's chest. It is still. He unwinds his white cotton blanket from his shoulders and wraps it round the child. The blood seeps through, an intricate, relentless, creeping pattern of black on white, then white on black. Fukanbuggrit. Fukanbuggrit.

Thomas Kayne gathers up the crimson shroud and stands, trembling under the dead weight. The child's head tips back. Thomas Kayne looks into its lifeless green eyes. And then he howls.

Daniel stretched out his hand and took Rachel's.

"I'm so sorry."

Her fingers gripped his. "I think I went mad for a while," she said quietly.

They sat together in silence for a long time. Daniel willed her not to let go of his hand.

"The man you live with …"

"Kamal Sharif."

"How does he … ?"

"Fit into the picture? I wondered when you'd ask that."

"It's just – he seems so …"

"Different?"

"And you don't seem to have much in common. Why do you stay with him?"

"It's not worth explaining. You wouldn't understand."

"Tell me. I might."

She hesitated. "I've got no choice."

"No choice? Why? Is it money you need? I could lend you—"

"Of course not," she said, angrily.

"Then what?"

"I told you, you wouldn't understand."

"He can hardly be keeping you chained up. You must have a choice."

"Just leave it."

"Tell me. Please. I want to understand."

"There's something I need from him."

"What? Security? A home? Bales of cloth? What?"

"A child."

"You need his child? You stay with someone like Kamal – you live with that – how can you need someone's child? You must be crazy!"

"What the fuck do you know?" she shouted, snatching her hand away from his.

"Enough to know that you're out of your mind. You're throwing your life away – for an unborn child by someone you can't bear to be with."

"Shut up!" Rachel put her hands over her ears.

"Someone's got to tell you."

"Oh yes! And that someone has to be you, I suppose? You – who've made such an obvious success of your life! You, who – who – had a choice – who had love and chose a life of – of – mediocrity and lies. Your lover didn't die. He's still out there somewhere."

"We're not talking about me."

"Why not? Who's making up these rules? At least I'm trying to hold on to something. I don't go around pretending Tahir never existed. Pretending to be someone I'm not."

"You don't have to pretend. You've turned into someone you're not."

"What's that supposed to mean?"

"Look at you – how long can you mourn someone? How many years has it been? What's the point?"

"What's the point? How dare you ask me what the point is? Who the fuck do you think you are?"

"A friend."

"I didn't ask for your friendship."

"Friends don't have to be asked."

"What is this – this – Charlie Brown psychobabble?"

Daniel put his head into his hands and laughed. "Oh, God. I'm sorry."

After a while, Rachel spoke, her voice no longer saturated with anger.

"I don't suppose there's anyone who'd understand what I've done."

"I want to, though. Really."

"Tahir was buried while I was at the clinic, having it confirmed that I'd lost the baby. I had no one to grieve with. For Tahir or the baby that he'd wanted so much. I had to mourn alone while his family closed ranks."

"What did you do?"

"Nothing. I checked into a small hotel in the city, went to bed and waited to die. I hoped I'd get some infection from the hospital that would finish me off, but that must have been the one occasion that year that they sterilised their instruments properly.

"I don't know when it was – I had lost all track of time – but one day Tahir's brother came to see me. I hadn't met him before – he'd been away on business when I arrived in the country. He seemed to know about Tahir and me. He was missing him dreadfully too. And that was it, really."

"That was what?"

"How I ended up with Kamal."

"Tahir's brother?"

"Maybe he saw me as some kind of connection with his brother. And I …"

"You wanted his child. A blood link to Tahir."

"Do you still think I'm out of my mind?"

"I don't know. I'm not sure I know anything any more."

"I thought that if I came here again – saw where he died – it might take some of the pain away – give me the strength to leave – but it hasn't."

"And the search for Thomas Kayne?"

"It's what Tahir and I started together. Maybe it's all about finding family."

"But you've got a family. What about your parents?"

"My father wrote his only letter to me last year to inform me – in three typed lines, I think it was – that my mother had died of a heart attack, that he blamed me for causing the stress that killed her, and that I and my black bastard could go to hell."

"But there was no child."

"I know. He can't have opened any of the letters I sent. Or let her see any of them."

"God, that's awful," whispered Daniel. He reached for her hand again and squeezed it.

"So how can I leave?" she asked at last, taking her hand from Daniel's and wiping the tears from her face. "What's there to leave for?"

"I don't know – the rest of your life?"

"What life?" she asked quietly.

"Come on. You're still young, you've got a huge talent. That voice ..."

"That voice! Do you know when I last sang anything? It was that time at Oxford. I barely talk these days, let alone sing."

"You're talking now."

"I'll go back to Kamal, you know. While there's still some hope of a baby."

"Do you feel anything for him?"

"For Kamal? I don't really think about it."

"Is that fair?"

"Is what fair?"

"Making love to him just to—"

"I don't make love to him."

"But I thought that—"

"I make love to Tahir."

"That's worse."

"Kamal doesn't do anything that he doesn't want to do. You don't get to be one of the wealthiest men in the country by doing anything for no reason."

"So what does he get out of it?"

"I don't know. Power? Consolation? Someone to help around the shop? It's not exactly something we discuss. But there'll be something, don't you worry."

"But what kind of life is that – for either of you? What about love?"

"What about it?"

They continued to sit side by side, listening to the noises of the night. At last Rachel got up.

"Good night, Daniel." She bent down and kissed him. He felt her hair brush his cheek. She smelled of frangipani.

"Where are you going tomorrow?" he asked.

"I don't know – along the river towards Jama, I think. I may as well carry on looking."

"Can I come with you?"

Rachel paused for a moment. "All right."

Father Seamus woke to the sound of an injured animal howling outside the gates of the compound. He looked at his watch. It was nearly four o'clock. He felt around for his dressing gown, a recent gift from Isabel. It ranked high in his list of favourite possessions, depicting as it did repeating patterns of orange weeping Virgin Marys. By the time he had found his torch and sandals, the noise had stopped.

He stood on the steps of the house peering out into the darkness. The animal, whatever it had been, must have crawled off to die in the bush. But as he turned to go back into the house he noticed a small mound by the gate. Father Seamus was used to gifts being brought to the Mission. He and Sister Mary Philomena often came home to find baskets of tomatoes and aubergines or paper twists of groundnuts by the gate, but he could not recall there being anything left there the evening before. He walked to the gate. There was a smell of blood. He frowned. They normally only received meat at Id al-Fitr. The priest knelt down and peeled away the layers of damp crimson cotton.

"Oh, Jesus Christ!" he whispered. "Jesus Christ!" He gathered up the bundle, holding the broken body of Abdulai Jammeh tight to his chest.

That evening, Father Seamus, his eyes red-rimmed, said a requiem mass in the Mission chapel. Abdulai Jammeh's family filled the first two rows. His mother, her head buried in her wrap, rocked backwards and forwards, sobbing hoarsely. His father sat staring blankly ahead, while his brothers and sisters, aunts and uncles, their faces grim and drawn, watched the priest conducting the unfamiliar ceremony. Susie sat weeping at the back of the chapel. Throughout the service, villagers came and went, shaking their heads as they filed past the body which Sister Mary Philomena had lovingly wrapped in a pure white shroud.

They buried the child at dusk in the small graveyard behind the chapel. Abdulai Jammeh took his place amongst the nuns and priests and the tiny scattering of converts who had lived and died in, or around, the Mission. The mourners gathered at the edge of the grave that his older brothers had dug that morning.

"Earth to earth, ashes to ashes, dust to dust," intoned Father Seamus, his eyes shut, as he threw handfuls of dry soil into the grave.

When he opened them, he noticed two people standing a little way away from the mourners. One of them was the policeman who had been called in from the town to investigate the incident. He was hovering by his car waiting to be given the money to fill it with enough fuel for the return journey. Fuck it, thought Father Seamus, suddenly angry. Let the eejit wait. He did not recognise the other onlooker who was half hidden behind one of the neem trees that shaded the older gravestones, but there were always a few curious spectators at his funerals, keen to witness the strange Catholic rituals.

Father Seamus embraced the dead child's mother and father, then stood watching them as they turned to follow the crowd that had slowly drifted away towards the village. Abdulai Jammeh's brothers shovelled the dry earth onto the body. It landed with a gentle thud. Susie sat, pale-faced, against a gravestone watching them.

"Are you all right, Susie?" Father Seamus asked.

"Yes. Thanks, Father." She stood up, brushing the dust off her skirt. "It's such an awful waste. I know all that stuff about a better place in heaven ..." Her voice trailed off.

"But Abdulai Jammeh was having quite a good time here on earth. I know. It's very hard. For everyone."

"Sister Mary Philomena's taken it very badly."

"We all have. Except perhaps our trusty constable over there who can't wait to get back to his desk and file his report – if he can borrow a pen off someone – saying he hasn't got the remotest idea how the boy died. Well, he can just wait a little longer."

"Oh, God!"

"What's the matter?"

"Shit – sorry, Father." Father Seamus followed Susie's appalled gaze. "I'll just go and see how Sister Mary Philomena is doing."

"Evening, Padre."

Father Seamus did not recognise the short, fat man with a sticking plaster on his cheek. "Can I help you?"

"Bit late in the day for gardening, isn't it?" The stranger reeked of whisky.

"Gardening?"

The man nodded at Abdulai's brothers who were shovelling the last of the earth into the grave. "Still, keeps them out of trouble, eh? Name's Newpin. Bob Newpin. And I'm after a phone."

"I've got a phone."

"Well thank fuck for that – 'scuse my French and all that."

"But as there aren't any phone lines in Brikaba, you'll be a long time trying to get through to anywhere. What is it you need?"

"My car's buggered. And I need to get back to the city pretty pronto. Bob Newpin is about to make a killing, yes siree!"

"It's a bit late to go anywhere. It'll be dark in a little while."

"I just need someone to pull out the bumper."

"If you give that policeman over there the money for fuel he'll probably take you into town."

"Policeman?" Newpin sounded worried. He looked over at the policeman who was leaning against his car smoking a cigarette. "Nah – you're all right. A couple of strong lads could probably do it. Here! Boys! Want to make a few bob for old Bob?"

"Leave them," said Father Seamus. "They've just buried their brother."

"What they do that for? Oh, I get you. Shame. Still – life's cheap here, eh?"

"What?"

"Life's cheap here. It's why they have so many kids. The will of Allah and all that. It's not like at home."

"This is my home."

"Well, you know what I mean."

"No, I don't think I do."

"Now, now, no need to get all uppity. I didn't mean any harm. It's all this living in the middle of nowhere. It takes away your sense of humour. Like this girl I met last night. Suddenly goes all peculiar on me for no reason." He took a swig from the bottle in his pocket. "You want a drink, Father?"

"No, thank you."

"Hold the headlines! 'Catholic priest says no to a drink!'"

"Look, we've had a long day here. Do you think you could go now. You could walk into town from here. And someone will fix your car in the morning."

"You couldn't put me up here then?"

"No, I'm sorry, I couldn't."

"I thought you lot were supposed to offer shelter to those in peril and all that."

"Normally I would. Just not tonight. I'm sorry. Town's that way."

"Just one night."

"No. Now good day to you."

"Fuck and bugger it!" shouted Newpin as Father Seamus turned towards the Mission house.

From the trees came a terrible sound. "Fukanbuggrit. Fukanbuggrit." Father Seamus spun round. An old man with wild grey hair was limping towards them. "Fukanbuggrit. Fukanbuggrit." His voice was filled with rage and anguish. "Fukanbuggrit. Fukanbuggrit," he cried, pointing his long finger straight at Newpin.

Newpin stepped backwards.

"My God!" said Father Seamus, looking from the old man to Bob Newpin. "You killed Abdulai Jammeh."

"Jammy what? And who's the mad geezer?"

"You killed the child and dumped him at the Mission."

"I never dumped him anywhere."

"But you did knock him down?"

"Look, what is this? Where I come from you're innocent until proved guilty. Now move out the way.

And you can stop pointing and waving your stick around an' all, you demented old tramp."

"He was drunk." Susie had come out of the house with Sister Mary Philomena and was standing looking at Bob Newpin. "Last night. At Uncle Peacock's. He tried to – he – he got really angry."

"What does that prove, exactly, missy? So I had a few drinks and went back to my lonely bed."

"What happened to your bumper?" asked Sister Philomena. "It looks to me as though you hit something."

"They taught you car maintenance at the nunnery, did they?"

"They did actually. It'll have been a slow puncture resulting from the bent bumper scraping against the tyre. It'll have got worse as you drove, which is why you've only just noticed the car's got a flat."

"Fukanbuggrit. Fukanbuggrit," the old man bellowed.

"Yeah, right, we heard you the first time," said Newpin, more nervous now. "Look. I never dumped anything anywhere. All right?"

"But you did hit the child," Father Seamus persisted. "Someone else must have carried the body to the Mission," he said, looking over at the old man.

"All right. I may've hit something. It was dark. It could've been a dog. And anyway, no one could prove anything. Grandpa over there's hardly going to sound convincing in court with his one word of gobbledegook. Now just bugger off, all of you."

Newpin grabbed one of the boys' bicycles and headed unsteadily towards the town.

Brighton, June 12th 1998

POST CARD
THE ADDRESS TO BE WRITTEN ON THIS SIDE

I trust the Foreign Office
waited until your french
was fluent before
transferring you to Spain.
I wouldn't like to think
of it doing anything
remotely sensible. My Italian's
fading fast. Ironically, my
Bakawa isn't.
Have some tapas for me. R x

Daniel Maddison
FCO Madrid
c/o King Charles St
London SW1A 2AH

Alec Moss pressed his fingers to his temples and scrunched up his eyes. Since his revelation about Isatou he had been beset by simultaneous feelings of joy, contrition and fear and was finding this an exhausting and confusing state in which to function. He shook his head in an attempt to clear it and pressed the button on his desk. After a few moments, Sandra Didsbury came into his office.

"You haven't seen Daniel, have you, Sandra?"

"That's just what I was going to ask you myself, sir. He's a dark one, that boy. I'd never have expected him to go AWOL. He's obviously found himself a nice local girl up in Brikaba. I told him no good would come of it, going away without me, but would he listen?"

"I take it that means no."

"It does, I'm afraid, sir."

"Sandra, how many times have I told you there's no need to call me sir?"

"I know, sir, but with your patrician good looks and air of elegant sophistication, I just can't stop myself."

"Is there anyone you don't flirt with, Sandra?"

"Ooh, sir, now you're being unkind. Of course there is." She paused for a moment to muster up an example or two. "There's that horrible little businessman for starters. You know, the one with the Bobby Charlton hairdo and the teeth that look like they belong to someone else. Bob whatsisname."

"Funny you should say that."

"Funny as in ha-ha or as in peculiar, sir?"

"Definitely not ha-ha, I'm afraid. That call you put through to me this morning – apparently he's caused an accident up-country. Some nun or other radioed the VSO people down here and they passed the message on. Len Barling's dealing with it."

"It never rains but it pours. Speaking of which, sir, I reckon your golf will be called off tomorrow. Baboucar tells me the weather's about to break. Which is what my heart will do if that Daniel doesn't show his beautiful face pretty soon. Is there anything else you wanted, or shall I get back to business?"

"No, that's it for now, Sandra. Let me know as soon as you hear from Daniel."

Alec could not help smiling as she click-clacked out of the room on her shiny high heels. He was grateful, now more than ever before, for his secretary's unfailing good humour. Life at the High Commissioner's residence was becoming grimmer by the day. He had moved into one of the guest rooms, but still found himself subjected to a daily bombardment of abuse from Fenella. To some extent, this was a relief. His feelings of guilt were such that, had she wept even once more, his resolve might have weakened. Luckily, after her immediate and uncharacteristic outpouring of grief, she had reverted to vitriol of such force that even Alec, well used to her verbal jousting, was left reeling. Despite all the upheavals, he was glad that her interest in bridge appeared undiminished. He hoped that her Scandinavian friend was someone that she was able to confide in.

There was a knock at the door.

"Have you got a moment, Alec?"

"Come in, Len. Everything all right?"

"Not exactly, no."

"Well – spit it out then."

"There's a Catholic priest sitting in my office."

"Erm, Len, I know you're United Reformed or something equally low church but I hardly think that the presence of a Catholic priest constitutes a major problem – not with that accident up-country and everything."

"It's about that accident. Seems it's rather worse than we'd thought. This priest – Father Seamus – is saying that Bob Newpin ran over a young boy."

"Christ! That's all we need. Is he badly injured?"

"He's dead."

"Dead? So why didn't this Newpin fellow report the accident himself? Where is he?"

"We don't know. And anyway the priest says he's denying killing anyone."

"Were there witnesses?"

"Just the one, apparently. An old man." Barling consulted the scrap of paper he was holding. "A Thomas Kayne."

"So where is this witness?"

"Back in the bush, according to the priest."

"What's he doing in the bush, for God's sake?"

"He didn't say."

"Look – get hold of Newpin," said Alec irritably. "This needs clearing up – and sooner rather than later."

"It's lucky it was a local child."

"What?"

"Newpin would really be up shit creek if he'd hit one of those Baptist missionary kids that run wild up there, or a VSO or something. With any luck he'll be able to give the family a couple of hundred lamasi and call it a day."

"What?"

"Call it a day. Are you OK? Not got that ear

infection again? And another thing – the visa office has gone to pot."

"What?"

"You need to get that ear looked at, Alec. It's Isatou Jammeh – you know, the senior administrator. She's gone into a real spin about something or other. Weeping and wailing like a banshee. No one's getting any work done. I'll get Sandra to sort it out, if that's OK with you – she's got a way with the locals."

"My ears are burning – what's that you said?" asked Sandra who had been on her way to re-apply her lipstick.

"Isatou Jammeh is having hysterics in the visa office. Sort her out, will you? A verbal warning should do the trick."

"Are you all right, sir?" asked Sandra.

"It's OK, he's got a problem with his ears."

"There's nothing wrong with my fucking ears, you racist idiot!"

Len stared at Alec in amazement. "What did you say?"

"I said there's nothing wrong with my fucking ears."

"No. After that."

"'You racist idiot'," said Sandra helpfully.

"Look, I know you've been having a bit of a bad time of it lately, what with Fenella and the Finn and stuff, but really. There's no need to be offensive."

"If anyone's being offensive round here, Len, it's you. I should have said something months ago."

"I'll be off to see to Isatou Jammeh now, shall I?" asked Sandra.

"No. Thanks. I'll go."

"You?" asked Len incredulously.

"Yes, me. Sandra, could you give the priest a cup of coffee and my apologies. Tell him I'll be there in a few minutes."

"No problem, sir. I might ask him if he's seen Daniel while I'm about it."

"Why should he have seen Daniel?"

"It's that nice Irish priest from Brikaba, isn't it? The one Daniel went up-country to stay with. I saw him come in earlier. Nearly didn't recognise him in his posh cassock."

Alec set off for the visa section. He was halfway down the corridor when a thought struck him. Len Barling's comment about Fenella and the Finn and 'stuff'. What exactly was all that about?

It felt to Daniel as though they had woken up after a wild storm. There was an eerie stillness that belied the turbulence of the night's gales, but the damaged trees of their souls were laid bare for both to see if they chose to. For now, neither did.

Rachel was already dressed and sitting on the veranda writing in her notebook. She looked up at him and smiled.

"Sleep well?"

"Yes, very, thanks. You?"

"Yes, thanks."

"Are you hungry? I don't know if this place does breakfast."

"No, I'm fine."

"Me too," said Daniel as Rachel turned back to her notebook. So it was Daniel's move. But move where and why? And how? "Sister Mary Philomena said there was a lovely stretch of river near here. Do you fancy trying to find it?" he asked hesitantly.

Rachel put her pen down. "I know the place. It's about a mile away from here. I went there once before. With Tahir."

"If you'd rather not …"

"No. I'd like to."

"You don't have to …"

"Come on. We can go on to Jama tomorrow."

Daniel followed her to the edge of the river. She walked purposefully. He caught a glimpse of her long bare legs as she scrambled down the riverbank. They sat side by side, watching the brown ripples lapping against the muddy banks. From time to time a bird that Daniel identified as some kind of kingfisher-thing darted across the water.

"*Halcyon malimbica*, the great white kingfisher. Isn't it lovely? Tahir told me that there were hippos here," Rachel continued. "Though we never saw any."

"Let's hope he was just making it up. They're terribly dangerous, aren't they? Don't they charge at people and trample them to death?"

"Only if you get between them and their young ones. Come on – let's walk a bit."

They walked side by side for a few miles along the riverbank to where the trees grew right down to the water's edge. From time to time, their hands brushed against each other lightly.

"It reminds me a bit of that stretch of the Isis. Near Port Meadow," said Daniel, idly tossing stones into the water.

"No pub, students or car park strewn with used condoms. But apart from that, it's identical."

"I said a bit," said Daniel, rather hurt.

"Watch out, Daniel!" Rachel shouted, her eyes suddenly wide with terror.

"What?"

"Behind you. A baby hippo."

Daniel spun round, setting off a tiny landslide as he did so. Rachel burst out laughing. She laughed and laughed until tears trickled down her cheeks.

"Sorry," she said, as soon as she was able to speak again. "I couldn't resist it."

"Very funny."

"God! I can't remember when I last laughed."

"You must have done, with Tahir."

"I don't know if I did, really. In a way, it was all too intense for laughter. Maybe if —"

"If what?"

"Nothing. I was talking to the manager earlier," Rachel said, changing the subject. "It seems that Thomas Kayne has been seen near here recently. So at least we know he's still alive."

"That's good."

"Is it? You know if we do find him, he won't know who I am."

"Does that matter?"

"So what am I doing it for?"

"I'm not really the person to ask. I'm the one who rationalised my relationship to shreds, remember."

"I'm sorry I said all that – about you and Jonathan."

"Why? It was true, mostly."

"Even so."

For a while they said nothing. Daniel glanced at Rachel. She was lying on her back now. He had an overwhelming urge to reach out and touch her. He could imagine the feel of the soft fair hairs on her arms, her smooth pale skin. He lay back and shut his eyes.

He woke with a start.

"Sorry," said Rachel, looking down at him. "You weren't supposed to wake up. It must have been all that laughing. I hope you don't mind." She caressed his face, her fingers following the contours of his eyes and jaw. Then she kissed him again. As she drew away, Daniel stretched out a hand, buried it in her hair and pulled her back towards him. He felt her fingers deftly unbuttoning his flies, then she knelt back up, her knees either side of his, and pulled her black dress over her head.

Much later, they rolled apart and lay with their fingers entwined looking up at the sky and the gathering rain clouds. Neither of them said anything. Rachel reached out for her dress, which she draped over their naked bodies, then she turned back to Daniel and rested her head on his chest. She shut her eyes and he stroked her hair until she fell asleep.

Fukanbuggrit. Fukanbuggrit. Thomas Kayne swipes blindly at the thorn bushes with his stick, breathless and bleeding. Fukanbuggrit he shouts back to the thunder. Fukanbuggrit. He can smell the river now. Hear it, already swollen. *Rafi, aradu, iska. Rafi, aradu, iska. Rafi, aradu, iska.* He clutches his head in his hands and turns it this way and that, while the words swirl round and round. *Rafi, aradu, iska.* River, thunder, wind. River, thunder, wind. He stumbles on. Babes in the wood, lying there. Hush – let them sleep. He touches the girl's arm. White and soft. Smooths out the black cloth. Don't stir. Don't stir things up. He looks up at the heavy sky. The rains are coming. The end is coming. He moves away into the darkness.

Isabel found two matching blue socks, folded them into a ball and tucked it into a corner of her battered leather case. It had been a strange week, she thought. What with Patrick stomping around like a child whose favourite toy has been confiscated and Father Seamus coming home in the evenings exhausted by the impenetrable bureaucracy of the High Commission and police.

"Has he gone, then?"

Isabel looked round and smiled at Patrick.

"About an hour ago. Sister Mary Philomena picked him up. She looked awful, I must say. At least a stone thinner."

"Has she been ill?"

"Just very upset. About that child."

Patrick looked blank.

"You know. The little boy who used to spend so much time at the Mission. The one you taught those rude rhymes to last time we were up in Brikaba. Abdulai Jammeh," said Isabel, trying to contain her exasperation. "The one that Seamus has been dealing with the police about. He's talked about it every evening."

"Of course. I must be going bonkers."

"Maybe not bonkers, Patrick love, but definitely distracted."

"He could have waited to say goodbye."

"He did. But as you didn't say when you'd be back, he couldn't very well have hung around all day. They wanted to get back up-country in daylight," said Isabel as she rummaged at the back of her wardrobe. She pulled out a grey jumper, sniffed it, and wrinkled her nose.

"This'll have to do, even if it does make me smell like a cellar."

"A seller of what?"

"A cellar. Damp and mildew and stuff."

"You see. I am going mad," said Patrick theatrically. "I'm losing the plot. Why's no one listening to me?"

Isabel took his arm, pulled him down onto the bed, sat down next to him and kissed him on the top of his head. She held his hand firmly and stroked it as she spoke.

"If by no one you mean me, Patrick, I am listening. I'm listening and packing. I've been listening to you for weeks. And I've been listening to Father Seamus and I've been listening to Sister Mary Philomena and to all our children on the phone." Isabel paused. She knew that if she let herself go on, it might be a while until she stopped. "So don't tell me I'm not listening. Please. It'll all turn out all right in the end."

"You see," he continued miserably.

"See what?" asked Isabel, shaking his hand in frustration. "See what, exactly?"

"You don't understand what I'm going through."

"Look, Patrick. I can see that this business with Alec and Isatou has upset you."

"Upset me? You make it sound as though it's some playground tiff. I knew you didn't understand," he finished petulantly.

"What exactly is there to understand? Isatou's pregnant. Alec's the father. They're going to have the baby. Just what is your problem?"

"There's no need to get cross with me."

Isabel shut her eyes. "I'm not cross. I'm just tired.

Tired of listening to your endless ranting and raving."
She knew as she said it that this was not what she had
meant to say.

"I've always ranted and raved. You've never minded
before."

Isabel did not reply.

"Have you?" Patrick persisted. "I do love you,
Isabel."

"I know. And I love you. I don't think that that's the
issue here."

"But you can't think it's natural."

"What?"

"Alec and Isatou."

"Patrick! This has got to stop."

"He's twice her age for a start."

"You may remember, if you stop to think about
somebody apart from yourself for just a minute, you
great egomaniac, that one of our daughters is married
to someone nearly twice her age. I don't remember you
having apoplexy over that at the time. You thought it
might be handy having a well-known theatre director as
a son-in-law. Useful for getting tickets when we're on
home leave."

"But this is different. It's an aberration!"

Isabel stared at her husband. A few hours later, as the
plane took off and she stared down at the disappearing
coast, she would think back to this moment. It was not
as though something had snapped, exactly. It had been as
though a wave of exasperation that had been gathering
strength over the years, a wave that had started as a
trickle of irritation, then a small swell of annoyance, with
occasional eddies of hurt, had suddenly crashed with all

its might on the shore of Patrick's unsuspecting head.

"Oh, grow up, Patrick!" she shouted.

Patrick stared at her, his eyes like those of a dog that has been suddenly kicked by a master who until then has shown it only kindness. At some point during their discussion, she must have let go of Patrick's hand. She could not remember when it was. She looked down at her empty hands, which were trembling slightly.

"You know what's the matter with you, Patrick? You just can't bear the fact that old Alec isn't acting to type – or rather the type that you assigned to him. Maybe he loves Isatou. Maybe she loves him. Who knows? Maybe he just fancies her and she quite likes him. Who knows that either? Maybe she wants a visa. Maybe he's having some mad mid-life crisis. Whatever they feel about each other, whatever decisions they make, they are two consenting adults who don't want or need your help or approval. What Isatou does with her life is none of your business."

"Of course it is. Alec's clearly exploiting her."

"I see. So speaks the man who's spent decades taking pictures of half-naked African women. Pictures that normal people would probably think should stay firmly on the top shelf."

A silence hung between Isabel and Patrick. A silence so unlike the comfortable space that usually existed between them that Isabel was shaken. She could see that Patrick was too. It was a silence that demanded filling, and filling with something that had never been said.

"You know I never ..." Patrick trailed off miserably.

"I didn't say you did."

"I've never been unfaithful to you, Izzy."

"I know."

"I promise."

"I said I know."

"I didn't think you minded. All the photography, I mean."

"I didn't think I did."

"Oh my God. That's why you're leaving me? Please, Isabel. Please don't. I love you."

"Oh, Patrick." Isabel began to laugh then stopped as she saw the fear in his eyes. "You know I'm going because I promised Catherine I'd be there when the baby's born. I've left it pretty late as it is. She could go into labour any minute. After the last one nearly showed up in the hospital car park. And I want to see the other children too."

"But you'll come back?" Patrick asked nervously.

"Of course I will. How could you doubt that I would?"

"That stuff you just said."

"Well, maybe it needed saying. Even if I didn't know, for a long time, that it did need saying. And maybe you should think about it for a bit. It'll give you something to do while I'm away. Now come and give me a hug before I go."

They stood in front of each other. Patrick looked into her eyes as though searching for some guarantee of her safe return. Then he took her in his arms. Isabel felt his mouth near her ear. The hairs on the back of her neck prickled. She supposed there would be time, if they were quick, before the taxi arrived. Most of her packing was done.

"I'm sorry," he whispered, his voice cracking. His arms tightened around her and he wept.

Alec took a deep breath and rang the bell. There was no reply. He took a step backwards and looked up at the windows. Various lights were on. Behind one set of curtains, a TV screen flickered. He rang the bell again. This time he heard the sound of footsteps and a slight snuffling noise as someone peered through the spy hole. A chain was removed and the door opened.

"Alec?" Len Barling looked nervous. "Come in. Long time no see. Socially speaking, I mean. Jackie!" he called out with a jollity that sounded somewhat forced. "It's Alec."

"I'm not disturbing you, am I?"

"Not at all. Not at all. Jackie and I were just looking at an old holiday video. The Red Sea."

"The diving trip?"

"That's the one," said Len, looking a little more relaxed now, and rather pleased that Alec should have remembered something about one of their many exotic holidays.

Jackie Barling came clattering into the hall on a pair of fluffy mules. She looked about as worried as her husband. News of Alec's uncharacteristic outburst had clearly made its way into the Barling household. She smiled at him warily.

"You're looking lovely as ever," lied Alec, kissing her on the cheek.

Jackie blushed, relieved at the revival of his old self. "Anyone for a G and T? Alec? Len?"

"Thanks, that would be lovely," replied Alec.

Jackie Barling had the reputation of mixing the

most potent gin and tonics in the region. Alec reminded himself to drink it slowly. He would need a clear head this evening. Len led the way into the lounge, sat him down and went to help his wife with the drinks.

Through the window, Alec could see the outline of the residence. He rarely saw his house from this angle. It looked desolate and unwelcoming, as though the very bricks had absorbed the unhappiness of the occupants. As he had left to go next door to visit the Barlings, Fenella, tight-lipped and stony-faced, had announced that she was going to see her Finnish friend. He needn't wait up.

On the television in the corner of the room, a paused, blurred Len in a black and fluorescent green wetsuit and a mask appeared to be holding up some kind of dead sea creature. Alec got up to have a closer look at a photograph on the mantelpiece. It was of the Barlings' only child, the improbably named Pearl. The acne-embossed teenager grinned out at him, her mouth a fortress of metal. Orthodontics, mused Alec. How does one decide to go into that? He did not recall his careers master ever having mentioned it as an option. Perhaps life would have been a lot simpler if he had. But would he really want life simple again?

"Here you are." Jackie handed him a large glass. "Chin chin."

"Yes, er, cheers."

"It's a lovely one that," said Jackie after a while.

"Yes, super. Just how I like it. Good and strong."

"I meant the photograph. It only arrived last week."

"Oh, yes. Very nice. She's a lovely girl."

"She's doing ever so well at her new school," said

Jackie, picking up the picture and gazing at it fondly. "It's really marvellous. They have ponies, you know."

"Do they indeed?"

"And fabulous sports facilities. Lacrosse and tennis."

"Jackie, love. I'm not sure that Alec is all that interested in schoolgirls in gymslips."

"Len, really!" she giggled.

The three of them sat in uncomfortable silence. For a moment, Alec wondered if he should go on. After all, Isatou wasn't even sure that she wanted to go to England. But there was so much he wanted her to see. Trains for a start. She'd love them. And escalators and garden centres and country pubs. Though come to think of it, how could he really know what she would like? He knew so little about her, really. But he wanted to know much more. After a while, Alec cleared his throat.

"Visas, Len. You must be something of an expert."

Len's face lit up. "I'll say so."

"I need a bit of advice."

"Fire away, mate."

"I know I ought to know this, but it's been a long time since I've been at that end of things. If, say, one had a local fiancée who might conceivably want to go to Britain sometime. To see if she liked it, say. Just for a visit, sort of thing. How easy would it be to get a visa for them?"

"Bloody hard if I've got anything to do with it."

"Why's that?"

"I can smell them a mile off if they're not genuine. I've a nose like a terrier." Len Barling was in his stride now and Alec realised, with some relief, that he would need little prompting. "They get a jolly good grilling from me, I can tell you. It's all in the questions you ask. You keep them apart, of course. Like that TV show – what's it called – *Mr and Mrs*. Ask them about each other's tastes in music, films – not that you get films here, and the music's awful, but you know the kind of thing I mean. Ask for letters, proof of their 'love', what their intentions are. Half the time, it's all a set-up. It's only a marriage in name. They don't ever see each other again once they're in the UK. If they get through immigration there, of course. There's no guarantee of that, even if I do give them a visa."

"But what if they are genuine? If they really love each other."

"Hardly ever happens, guv'nor."

It must be the combination of the alcohol and the fact that Len was on home ground both personally and professionally, thought Alec, that had spawned this new, and not entirely welcome, mateyness.

"Another gin and tonic?" asked Jackie.

"No thanks. I'm still halfway through this one."

"Pringles? Japanese nibbles?"

"No, I'm fine, thanks."

Unasked questions hung in the air. Once or twice, Jackie appeared about to grasp one and ask it, but then seemed to think better of it. Len looked at him quizzically, frowning now and again, as though trying, and failing, to add two and two together, despite his very best efforts. Alec thought of Isatou. He thought of the way her smooth black skin had tightened over the bulge that would be their child. Would any of this have happened if she hadn't become pregnant, he wondered. Would their hearty, illicit coupling have grown into the precious, tentative love that now filled him with a joy and an optimism about the future that he had never felt before? Did it feel like that to Isatou? He could only hope so, with all his heart.

He looked up at the Barlings. They looked back at him, expectantly. In for a penny, thought Alec. "You've probably heard that things – that Fenella is …"

"So you do know," Jackie started. She sounded relieved. "We weren't sure if—"

Len coughed and she stopped. Alec looked out at the silhouette of his house and then back at the Barlings.

"It's Isatou. Isatou Jammeh. We're going to get married. If she'll have me, of course."

Jackie Barling's eyes, bulbous at the best of times, looked as though they were about to part company with their sockets. Len frowned, trying hard to assimilate this information that made no sense whatsoever.

"And we're going to have a baby." Alec heard a strangled gasp but could not work out from which of them it emanated. "So I suppose you'll be giving us one of your special goings-over – your *Mr and Mrs* thing. I hope you won't be too hard on us, Len."

My darling Patrick,

Here, as promised, a picture of your fourth granddaughter, as yet unnamed. I'd tell you some of the names on the shortlist but I'd hear you snort with derision from here, so I won't. I'm rather enjoying a life free of derisory snorting.

She is, it goes without saying, the most beautiful baby in the world, tied equal, of course, with her elder brother (who has mercifully not yet understood just how much his life is about to change with the arrival of his sister) and all her cousins. Catherine is coping wonderfully. Ned spends most of his spare time at her house. He is as delighted as the rest of us with his new baby. Their rather unconventional lifestyle seems to suit them all.

I could use this opportunity to make a point about unconventional lifestyles and enquire as to whether you have congratulated Alec and Isatou yet, as you promised me you would when I last telephoned, but I won't.

I've seen all the children now. Spent a day with Anna in Winchester last week and met up with Celia at the Tate the other day. Sarah and Eliza came down to Catherine's on Sunday. Plus partners and all their children. Chaos, but fun. You'd have loved it. I wish you could have been there, even though you'd have got the children hopelessly overexcited before bedtime and probably dropped a couple of them on their heads. I'll be spending a few more days with each of them before I come back.

I went to stay with Joe last week, as I told you on the phone. He sends his love. Says that he really will write us a letter one day but couldn't be drawn on when that day might be. Lucy seems to have managed to curb some of his more slovenly habits. I noticed that he has learned to hang up his towels after his bath rather than leaving them in a damp pile on the floor. And I even got one cup of tea in bed. Maybe if I'd been a bit more like Lucy, you too could have been civilised.

Lucy is a sweetie. Not at all unlike her cousin Daniel in looks – equally beautiful – with the same fine features and high cheekbones. And those lovely dark blue eyes, of course. I didn't mention it on the phone – we were cut off before I had the chance – but a friend of hers came to dinner while I was staying with them, and it turned out he knew Daniel. They were all at Oxford together. Jonathan Rosen. Tall and blond – very Aryan, ironically. So there I was, eating my crème brûlée, going on about what an incredible coincidence it was, all of us knowing each other, when I realised that Lucy had obviously set the meeting up. I felt such a stupid old woman.

I couldn't think why she'd gone to all the trouble of getting Jonathan round while I was there, until I saw the way he looked when I talked about Daniel, and the kinds of questions he asked about him, and suddenly I knew that they must have been lovers. You see, I was right. I always am. About that kind of thing, if nothing else.

Anyway, we ended up talking so much that Jonathan missed his train back to Oxford. Lucy played some of his recordings – he was sweetly modest about them, but he shouldn't have been. I'm going to buy a couple of tapes and bring them back. I think you'd love them. And then Lucy and Joe went to bed (Joe had clearly exhausted himself by the picking up of towels earlier) and Jonathan and I carried on talking. He's charming and good-looking

*like Daniel – but where Daniel seems to struggle, to find
it hard to say what he really thinks, even to know what
he really thinks, Jonathan has a kind of quiet certainty
about him. Anyway, it got to about four in the morning
and we were still talking, and then we hatched a plan. It's
not without its risks – it could all end in tears – but I think
it will be all right. It should be all right. And before you
ask, no, I'm not going to tell you what it is – you'll find
out soon enough.*

*It was good to hear your voice on the phone yesterday.
I do miss you and your dreadful ways, you know,
whatever I may have said the day I left.*

   With love,
   Isabel xx

Kamal Sharif folded the letter and carefully put it back inside the envelope. Then he tipped his chair back and sat staring past his computer screen. So it had happened at last. He had always known it would, of course, but not now; it should not have happened so soon. His throat tightened, and his eyes blurred for a moment. A second death – of sorts.

He wondered if she would come to see him before she left. He doubted she would. What was there to say to each other now, after all those years during which nothing had really been said, nothing kind at least, but so much had been understood.

Faysal had always had his reservations about the whole thing, he knew that – but then Faysal had not loved Tahir as they had. Had they done wrong to each other – by each other? Probably. Almost certainly. He had never lied. Just not told the whole truth, but then he was sure that she had not either. Anyway, it was too late now. It was over.

"There's a man to see you downstairs in the shop."

Kamal looked up to see his cousin Yussuf standing in the doorway. He picked up the letter, held it as though about to tear it in half, then changed his mind, put it in the drawer and locked it. He walked to the window of the gallery and looked out over the shop. It was that little entrepreneur. "What does he want?"

"He wouldn't say. Just said he was in a hurry and had to see you urgently."

"Send him up." Kamal lit a cigarette.

Bob Newpin panted up the stairs. "Blimey – you

ought to get a lift put in here. Could be a bit dodgy, though, with all the power cuts you have here."

"We have our own generator."

"Course you do. Course you do, mate. Big cheese like yourself."

"What can I do for you?"

"It's more what I can do for you, if you get my meaning."

"I don't."

"Look, I'll get straight in at the deep end. I'm in a bit of a hurry, actually. Got a meeting with your chum, the Minister of Tourism, in half an hour. Forget the timeshare down here – that's old news. Up-country is where it's at. In Brikaba. Barbies in the bush, moonlight cruises with the crocodiles, visits to a genuine mud hut, poor but happy locals, the whole damned caboodle. We're looking megabucks here, Kammy my boy, megabucks."

"Really?" Kamal's eyes narrowed. Something Faysal had mentioned to him last week gradually made more sense. "Brikaba. There was some kind of incident there recently, wasn't there?"

Bob Newpin flushed a deep purple.

"Look, what is it with this place? There's no proof. Not a sausage. If I hit anything – and I'm not saying I did, mind – it was a dog and as dogs seem to be bred for kicking here, I can't see what all the fuss is about. That's my story and I'm sticking to it. Now about the timeshare – you coming in with me? Tundra Jy's going to want some facts and figures."

Kamal stubbed out his cigarette in a heavy onyx ashtray. "I'm sure he is."

"Is that a yes, then?"

"I'm certainly interested. In getting some facts and figures to him."

"That's fucking brilliant! You won't regret it, you know."

"I don't suppose I will."

"So I'll tell the Minister, will I?"

"You do that."

"Is that it, then?"

"For now. Yes. You can find your own way out of the shop, can't you? I've just got to make a couple of phone calls." Kamal turned away to avoid Newpin's outstretched hand.

"Yeah, no probs. No probs at all, mate. Arrivyderchy."

Kamal sat down again at his desk. The revulsion he had felt for the fat little entrepreneur had taken his mind off the letter. He unlocked the drawer, took it out and read it once more. So the search was off. She had not said why. Perhaps that was one ghost she had laid to rest. He scanned her words for clues about her decision. There were none. Her words were as impassive as her face had been. Impassive, but beautiful. He would miss that face – with its range of expressions from calm contempt to passionate fury. Had there been other expressions in between? Maybe that first time, when they had found some kind of bitter-sweet consolation in each other, when they had made love silently and desperately, each raging with grief. But no – not since then.

There was only one thing she had wanted from him. He had always known that. And there had only been one thing he had wanted from her. Her presence – her unquenchable grief and her anger – which kept the memory of his brother alive, did not allow it to get subsumed under the minutiae of his ever more successful business dealings. He tore the page in half, then into tiny pieces. The link was finally severed.

Kamal picked up the phone and dialled.

"Yes. The Minister of Tourism please. Ah! Tunde! It's Kamal. Fine, fine. And you? Good … Yes, I know. He should be with you in about five minutes. He's just been here …" Kamal laughed. "Well, you guessed right. What's the expression they have – not with a bargepole … and anyway, he won't be at large for much longer … Just humour him for half an hour or so. That should give me time enough to sort something out. No … no … good – I'll see you for tennis on Saturday. Yes, I will and send mine to your wife too."

Kamal put down the phone. He flicked through his diary and dialled again.

"Police chief please. Yes … yes, that's right … Tell him it's Kamal Sharif … No, I won't ring back later." Kamal waited as his call was put through. "Modou! Good to talk. I know. It's been a long time. Too long … Sure … that would be great … Friday week. Come down to the beach house. Bring the family. Listen, in the meantime, could you do me a favour – us all a favour really. You know that hit and run incident in Brikaba? …"

Brighton, June 4th 1999

POST CARD

THE ADDRESS TO BE WRITTEN ON THIS SIDE

Still waiting for the Summer
to come to Brighton — I envy
you the Spanish sun.
Did I forget to congratulate
you on your promotion to
First Secretary?
If so, sorry, and congratulations.

R x

Daniel Mastolisan
FCO Madrid
c/o King Charles St.
London SW1A 2AH

It had stopped at last. The rain that had collected on the umbrellas dripped heavily onto the chairs and tables of the café, steam rose from the puddles on the uneven concrete floor, the air was thick with the promise of another storm. There was something different about the smell here now, something fresh and pungent. Daniel looked up at the charcoal grey sky. He felt water seeping through the soles of his shoes and gradually making its way up the legs of his trousers. He wondered if he had time for a drink before the rains started again, and hesitated while he tried to gauge which table would be the least sodden.

Ibraima came out of the kitchen and surveyed the damp scene. He picked up the chairs, shook them, then wiped them down. He tipped away the soggy cigarette butts that bobbed in the ashtrays and flapped the umbrellas open and shut, sending out a shower of raindrops.

"Mr Daniel! *Salaamalekum!* I didn't see you there. Come, come. This is the driest table. It's been a long time. How was Brikaba?"

Daniel shook Ibraima's hand warmly. "*Malekum-salaam.* Good to see you again. Brikaba was fine. Very – er – different. From here."

"Your usual?"

"Yes please, that would be lovely."

Daniel looked out over the swollen, grey river. Different. It had certainly been that. He remembered the way that Rachel had got up and pulled on her black dress. The way she had gone down to the river and splashed water on her face, the way that she had walked back towards him, smiling slightly. Neither had spoken as they set off back towards the hotel in darkness, listening to the sound of the frogs and the thunder. When the rain started to fall, they sheltered under some trees, standing very close to each other, but not quite touching.

He had wanted to say something to her, to make some kind of sense out of what had happened, why it had happened, but as usual the words would not come. Had she been thinking about Tahir? He would never know. He did not even know what, or who, he had been thinking of. Outside their rooms, Rachel had hesitated, then put her arms round him, drawing him in close to her and kissing him gently on his forehead. "Good night, Daniel," she had whispered, before going into her room and closing the door behind her. And though she never said anything, he sensed that her search for Thomas Kayne was over.

The rain continued to fall and the roads began to flood. If they did not leave soon, their journey would become very unpredictable. They travelled back in a World Food Programme vehicle, a lift arranged by the somewhat bemused hotel manager. The two foreigners had clearly not behaved as he had anticipated. The driver had very little English, and as Rachel had not volunteered any Bakawa, they had not had to make much conversation with him. As they neared the city, and out of view of the driver's mirror, Daniel had tentatively taken her hand.

"What are you going to do now?"

"I don't know yet."

"If there's anything I can do …"

"Thank you. I'll be fine. Really, Daniel." She had squeezed his hand, then let it go.

Ibraima placed the tiny cup and saucer in front of

Daniel. "You look tired. All that travelling can be quite exhausting. And the roads must have been bad – with all that rain. You must have had quite a journey."

"I have," said Daniel, with feeling. "Look, Ibraima. You know everything that goes on in this place, don't you?"

Ibraima laughed. "I wouldn't say that, exactly, but go on. Try me. What is it you want?"

"The Sharif brother you mentioned once. The one who died …"

"Tahir Sharif? There aren't many people here who haven't got a story to tell about him."

"A story?"

"He was quite a – what do you people call it – a character. Quite a character. Brilliant – but then all of the Sharif brothers are in their own ways. There's Kamal and his cloth business – the man with the golden key, they call him. There aren't many doors he can't open – and Naveed – the doctor in the States – what was it you asked?"

"About Tahir."

"Yes, sorry. Tahir." Ibraima sat back expansively. "What do you want to know about him?"

"What was he like?"

"Brilliant, as I said. Very attractive – but you'll know that."

"How come?"

"You've seen Kamal, haven't you?"

"Kamal?"

"They were twins."

"Twins," repeated Daniel, trying to assimilate this new piece of information.

"Identical – in looks at least. That Tahir was a wild

one. What do you call that character in a book who had two personalities?"

"Jekyll and Hyde?"

"Jekyll and Hyde, that's it. Take him out of his laboratory, and that man sure knew how to have a good time." Ibraima laughed appreciatively. "You just have to look round some of the primary schools here."

"I'm afraid you've lost me."

"His reputation wasn't just for his malaria research."

"I know this must sound a bit dim, but I still don't get it."

"Let's just say, he put it about a bit. Isn't that the expression? I don't know exactly how many children he fathered. And that's just here. I've no idea what he was up to while he was in the UK. But they say a leopard doesn't change his spots. Another Lebanese coffee?"

Daniel frowned. "No thanks, Ibraima."

"Anything else you want to know?"

"What about Kamal? What did they have in common – apart from their looks of course?"

"The same kind of charisma, I suppose. But Kamal's quieter, much quieter."

"No hordes of illegitimate children, then?"

"No any kind of children, sadly."

"What do you mean?"

"There was an outbreak of mumps when we were at school – he was the year above me."

"Mumps?"

"That's the right word, isn't it?" Ibraima looked worried. "The disease where your face swells up and it can be bad news for men."

"Yes, that's right. Mumps. So what are you saying?

That Kamal is infertile? How on earth could you know that?"

Ibraima shrugged his shoulders. "It's just one of those things. I can't remember how I know. Why, does it matter?"

"No, no, of course not."

"You haven't drunk your coffee. It'll be cold now. I'll get you another one."

"No, don't worry."

"I insist."

"Well you have one too, in that case."

Daniel watched as Ibraima ducked under the dripping umbrellas and made his way into the kitchen. He stared out across the river. A few weeks ago, he would have known what to do. He would have gone straight to Rachel, full of righteous indignation, and told her everything – that Kamal would never be able to father the child she so desperately wanted, that she was wasting her life. That there would be no blood tie with the past. But not now. Now he knew that life was rarely that black and white. He looked up. The clearest anything could ever get was probably the colour of the lowering sky above him.

Alec hovered outside the open door. From where he was standing, he could just see the suitcase on the bed. Every so often an article of Fenella's clothing would land in it as though self-propelled. From the force with which the clothes were thrown, he had little doubt what mood his wife was in. He took a tentative step forward. He could see her now, angrily folding up her blouses, then flinging them into the case. As they soared the distance between wardrobe and case, they unfurled, their arms flailing like those of a person drowning.

"Can I help?" he asked weakly.

"Go fuck yourself."

"That's a no then?"

A shoe sailed through the air and hit him on the side of his head. He managed to duck just in time as its partner hurtled towards him. He bent down miserably and picked the shoes up, then laid them carefully on the bed, the soles touching.

"Look, Fenella. It doesn't have to be like this."

"I'm not listening." She began to hum loudly – it sounded like that battle song from *Les Misérables*. She'd always been one for musicals.

"Fenella – listen to me for a moment. Please. You don't have to move out now. I'm quite happy in the spare room. There's no great hurry. There's plenty of time to work something out that is good for both – all – of us."

The humming grew louder.

"And then there's Mimi."

The humming stopped abruptly. "If you think you'll ever see that dog again, think again. Come within fifty yards of her, and I'll kill you," she snapped.

"Couldn't I take her for the occasional walk or something? Please, Fenella. She's nearly fifteen. She won't be around that much longer."

"Well, you should have thought about that earlier, shouldn't you?"

"She's been part of my life for so long."

"Only half as long as I've been. But that didn't stop you, did it? You're more concerned about the dog than you are about me."

Alec detected a plaintive note in her voice surfacing through the scorn, and another wave of guilt swept through him.

"Look, Fenella, that's not true. I can't tell you how bad I feel about this – this whole thing."

"Like hell."

"I do."

"Oh, you poor thing. Let's all feel sorry for poor little Alec Moss, shall we? Poor little Alec Moss who got so bored with his wife that he just had to swop her for someone less than half her age. Poor, poor thing."

Well, at least she was talking to him, thought Alec. It was better than those days of furious silence, punctuated by the odd, carefully selected, term of abuse. She had long stopped caring who overheard her and it was with some regret that he accepted that there were probably few things now that their staff, and their extended families, did not know about his anatomy. Fenella was on a roll now. He thought it only fair that he let her carry on uninterrupted.

"I'll make sure your career is over, you know. I'll make damned sure you don't get that knighthood you've been angling for. Sir Alec and Lady Isatou! Over my dead body! And, by the way, there won't be any romantic breaks for you and that fat black cow in the Dordogne. The house in France is mine, so don't even bother to get the solicitors involved or I'll take you to the bloody cleaners. You owe me that house – after all those years I've spent trailing round the world with you, entertaining for you, ruining my complexion in climates more suited to fucking monkeys than people, living in shit-holes like this because you're too fucking useless to ever get a decent posting. And I'm taking the Persian rug. It'd be wasted on her."

Fenella paused briefly and snapped the suitcase shut.

"And don't bother sending me an invitation to the wedding."

"I don't even know if she wants to marry me."

"Of course she wants to marry you. That's what they all want. You don't suppose she got pregnant by accident, do you? You always were naïve. I used to find it oddly charming. I can't think why now. They're scheming slappers, you know – just ask Len. It's not you, Alec. You could have been anyone, you know: any stupid bastard who's vain enough to think that a twenty year old would be interested in some late middle-aged, drooping has-been for anything other than a ticket out of here."

"We're not necessarily getting out of here."

"What's that supposed to mean?"

"Isatou's said she doesn't want to be too far from her family. Not while the baby's small, at least. And whether she marries me or not, we're going to bring up the child together."

"Oh spare me the Penelope bloody Leach. Do you

think I have the slightest interest in your future?"

"I was just trying to explain."

"Well, don't. And I'll have the photographs."

At least, Alec thought, she wanted to keep some of their memories of happier times.

"I'll enjoy sitting in our house in France, looking through them," she went on. "Then cutting them all up into tiny little pieces."

"Where are you going to go?" Alec asked, eyeing the suitcase.

"What business is it of yours?"

"Of course it's my business. You're my wife. I still care about you. I can't just watch while you walk out of here with nowhere to go."

"Oh, my heart bleeds for you."

"I do care. You really don't have to leave now."

"Take this," she said, pushing the case in his direction. "You might as well do something useful. For the novelty factor, if nothing else."

"Where do you want it?"

"By the front door. I'm being picked up in a few minutes."

"Who by?"

"By whom."

"By whom. Is it your Finnish friend?"

"Well done, Inspector Clouseau."

"That's very nice of her – to have you."

"Yes, isn't it?"

Alec heard the sound of a car pulling up outside. He walked over to the window and peered out. A pistachio-coloured open-topped sports car, bearing diplomatic number plates, was parked by the avocado tree. A pale-skinned blond man got out of the car and stood by it, looking at his watch. It was then that the penny dropped. He could almost hear it land and spin round and round before coming to rest. He turned slowly and stared disbelievingly at his wife.

"The Finn – Paavo – he's a man."

Fenella stared back at him, with a look of amused defiance.

"I never said he wasn't."

"You said you were going to Dakar with a girl friend."

"No. Correction. You said I was going to Dakar with a girl friend. I didn't feel I needed to put you in the picture, knowing how you always like to think you're right about everything."

"You must have been having an affair with that Finn for months."

"Years, darling."

"Years?"

"Two years. Near enough."

"You've been having an affair with him for two years?"

"And there were plenty of others before that. Remember that rather handsome driver we had in Syria?"

"Not Sidi?"

"Yes, that was him. I'd forgotten his name. We didn't exactly do much talking." She smiled, knowingly. "And your number two in Mauritania?"

"I don't believe you!"

"And that nice sixth-former on work experience in Lisbon."

"He was sixteen!"

"Seventeen, actually. Don't bother with the sanctimony. It doesn't suit you. And don't do yourself a disservice by trying to tell me that Isatou was your one and only peccadillo. You've been at it all the time we've been married."

The front doorbell sounded impatiently.

"Right. Well, we'll be off now. Me and Mimi. I'll send a van round for the rest of my stuff. And the rug and a few other knick-knacks that you won't be needing. What's the matter? The dog got your tongue?"

"She was," said Alec quietly.

"Who was what?"

"Isatou. My only – 'peccadillo'."

Fenella roared with bitter laughter. "Oh, don't be ridiculous."

"She was. I know I may have flirted a bit."

"A bit? You never kept your hands to yourself. Don't think I didn't notice. Me and everyone else in the southern hemisphere."

"It's the truth."

Fenella looked at Alec. "I wish you hadn't told me that," she said. Something in her voice had changed.

"About Isatou?"

The doorbell rang again. This time they heard Kaddy's footsteps, and the front door opening.

"No, you idiot," she said, reverting, with what sounded like relief, to her usual self. "God! How will I live without your sparkling intellect and razor-sharp wit? No. Don't answer. Just take the case down for me. Mimi! Here, baby. Come to Mummy."

Rachel moved silently through the house, her bare feet cool on the smooth marble floor. She opened the door to her bedroom. The shutters were closed and the room was warm and musty. For a moment, she was overwhelmed by a feeling of terrible tiredness. She lay face down on the bed and buried her head in the pillow. Even after more than two months, she could smell the familiar smell of cigarettes and expensive aftershave that lingered long after Kamal's regular night-time visits.

The two young sisters who cleaned the house and did some of the cooking had stared at her with big, curious eyes as she had let herself into the house, but said nothing. She wondered what Kamal had told them. Not to expect her back again, most likely. Faysal and Suhad had not looked surprised to see her when she had arrived at their house. Kamal must have warned them that she might turn up. They had been polite and kind, as usual. They had asked few questions, even though she knew that Kamal would have told them very little, if anything. He had kept away, as she had known he would.

Suhad was almost full term now. Sometimes, as the two of them sat together in the evenings, waiting for Faysal to come back from his office or from checking in a container at the docks, Rachel would see the baby kick through the folds of Suhad's exquisite silk maternity dress. She recognised the material. Knew from which of the bolts of cloth it had been cut. The first time she saw the baby move, she had wished, just for a moment, that she had not sent the letter. But it was done and now she was leaving. There would be no baby. She would just have to bear it. Somehow.

Rachel got up off the bed and opened the shutters. The afternoon sunlight filtered in. Everything was exactly as she had left it. Kamal could keep her books, though she knew that he had no patience with fiction. Her few clothes could go to the servants, though she doubted that they would have much use for her plain, shapeless, dark dresses. Her diary and enough clothes to see her through until she left were in the bag she had taken to Brikaba. There was only one thing she needed to salvage.

She reached up above her bed and took down the wooden carving that Tahir had bought her in the market in Brikaba. She traced her fingers along the surface of the two figures that were encircled by a decorated hoop of wood. She stroked the swollen breast and belly of the one, touched the round fruit held to her open mouth by the other. Then her fingers found the crack that ran across one side of the carving. She shut her eyes. She could see herself holding it on her lap in the car; remember her fingers tightening on the wood as the car had spun out of control. Only a surface crack. It had survived better than she had done.

Rachel closed the shutters. Then, very quietly, she opened the door that led into Kamal's room. Strange to think that in all the years in his house, she had never been into this room. She tried to remember if he had ever told her not to. She didn't think that he had. It was scrupulously tidy. She was not surprised. A few very tasteful ornaments, collected on his travels, were displayed in a tall glass cabinet. A cover of crimson silk embossed with hundreds of tiny mirrors enveloped the double bed in which she had never slept. She fingered the smooth shiny pieces.

On the bedside table was a single framed black and white photograph. It was of her and Kamal. One of Kamal's arms was draped round her shoulders. They were looking into each other's eyes and laughing. She picked it up and looked at it closely, trying to remember where it had been taken, when it was that she and Kamal had laughed together.

She gazed at the skilfully blurred background. Then, as though she were looking at the photograph through developing fluid, she saw the surroundings come into focus. It was her room at Oxford. The evening before her concert. Of course it was not Kamal. She put the photograph back on the table. He must have found it amongst Tahir's possessions while she was in the hospital. Before he met her. It would have been the first image Kamal had had of her. Smiling, laughing, loving.

Curious, now, she went over to his desk. She hesitated for a few seconds, then opened the drawer. It was empty but for a thick leather binder. She took it out and slowly turned the pages. The sound of an electric saw interrupted her thoughts.

She walked to the window and looked out into the garden. A digger was parked on the lawn, ready to start work on the swimming pool. Two men she recognised as labourers that Kamal occasionally took on in the warehouse – one armed with a chainsaw, the other with an axe – were chopping down the frangipanis. One by one, the beautiful trees crashed to the ground and were hacked into pieces. The men tossed the mutilated stems and branches into a pile in a corner of the garden. The cream and pink flowers smiled bravely out of the carnage.

By the morning they would be brown and wilted.

Rachel swallowed. There was an aching lump in her throat. She walked into her bathroom, rummaged through a drawer and found a sharp pair of scissors. Then, sitting at Kamal's desk, she cut a neat square out of the hem of her dress. Next to the last entry – a piece of fine, dark red silk – she placed the small fragment of plain black cotton. Then she picked up the carving and walked out of the house.

Daniel watched her as she ate. She toyed lethargically with her bread, picking up the crumbs from the table one by one and placing them carefully at the side of her plate.

"Can I get you something else? More bread? Juice?"

"No, thanks."

"What time's the flight, again?"

"Three. Check-in's at one, but it'll be fine if we get there at two."

"Are you all packed?"

"Yes, thanks."

Susie's eyes were dull. An infected mosquito bite on her neck glistened with pus. Her light brown hair hung limply over her hunched shoulders. When Father Seamus had sent a message down to Daniel, asking whether he could put her up for a night and take her to the airport, he had mentioned that she was in need of a little care and attention. Looking at her now, that seemed something of an understatement.

A rather sombre Patrick had sat with Daniel over bottles of beer at Bakari's bar telling him about the child's death and the effect it had had on so many people. Apparently, though, Patrick had said, it wasn't all bad news. Someone, somewhere, must have pulled a couple of strings. Newpin had been arrested in town – hauled out of a meeting with the Minister of Tourism by two very large policemen, they said – and was now sharing a cell with a motley collection of thieves and pimps in the city prison awaiting trial at some unspecified date in the future.

Len Barling had given Daniel the official briefing on his first day back in the office. *That idiot child-killer Newpin's in the clink* had been his opening words. *Not a lot we can do about it,* he had concluded before stomping back into his office, muttering irritably about the world having gone completely mad.

Susie picked at a scab on her arm.

"I was really sorry to hear about Abdulai Jammeh," Daniel ventured.

"Thanks."

"I met him a couple of times."

"I know. He thought you were nice."

"You'll all miss him a lot."

"Not as much as his family will," Susie replied, pointedly.

"No, of course not. Of course not."

Susie was showing little inclination to leave the table and gather her belongings together.

"How long's your leave?" Daniel asked, steering the conversation onto safer ground.

"Six weeks. If I decide to come back."

"You will come back, won't you?"

"I don't know."

"I'm sure Father Seamus would want you to."

Susie looked directly at Daniel for the first time. "Do you think so?"

"He's always talking about you."

Susie's face became almost animated. "Is he?"

"He's obviously really impressed with your women's garden project."

"Oh, that," she replied dully, dragging herself to her feet and disappearing into the spare room. Daniel frowned. He had thought she would be pleased.

They drove in silence past the hotels. The tourist season was coming to an end. Outside each hotel complex, crowds of holiday-makers swarmed towards the waiting coaches. Clad in batik shirts and clutching straw hats and wooden elephants (it did not seem to matter to them that elephants had never been seen in this part of Africa), they were clearly prepared to risk considerable discomfort to their sunburned bodies as they jostled for window seats. Several middle-aged women who probably had sensible teaching or secretarial jobs back in the real world were putting off boarding until the very last moment, disinclined to detach themselves from the firm and darkly toned embraces of their youthful partners. It was lucky, Daniel mused, that they would be out of sight, several thousand feet up in the air, before their 'boyfriends' moved in on the new arrivals. But then, what did he know about relationships? Maybe some of them would work out.

Images of Rachel flashed through Daniel's mind as he drove along the airport road. Though he did not know how, he had understood the moment she had let his hand go in the taxi that whatever had happened between them would never again be mentioned, that he would probably never see her again. He did not know where she was living or what she planned to do. And as for what she felt about those days in Brikaba, he had absolutely no idea.

While he negotiated the flooded potholes in the piece of wasteland that served as the airport car park, he spotted Patrick getting out of his car and adjusting his hat. It looked as though he might have had it washed in anticipation of Isabel's return – evidence, if any were needed, of how terribly he had missed her.

"Ah, Daniel! This is clearly the place to be. I've seen about six people I know already. And who's your delightful companion?" His mood had improved immeasurably in the last few days as Isabel's return had become ever more imminent.

"Susie Ashton," he replied, as she hauled her rucksack out of the boot of his car and leaned it against the back wheel. "She's a volunteer up in Brikaba."

"You must know our very dear friend, Father Seamus," Patrick continued amiably.

"Bye, Daniel. Thanks for the lift," said Susie.

"What did I say?" Patrick asked as he watched her desultory progress towards the airport building.

"Don't worry about it. Looking forward to Isabel coming back?"

"Is the Bishop a bigot?"

Daniel laughed. "Me too. Has she had a good time?"

"Seems so. You know what the post is like, though, and the phones always go up the creek as soon as the rains start. She rang last night. Said she had a surprise but then that thunder started – you must have heard it – the best storm yet – and the line went dead. One of the other daughters is probably pregnant. They're a fertile lot, those Redmond girls. Or maybe it's Lucy? That'd be a shock for Joe, the lazy sod," he added affectionately. "Hey, isn't that your mystery cloth woman?"

"What?"

"There, getting out of that taxi."

Daniel looked round. "Rachel!" He ran up to her as the taxi drove off.

She brushed the hair from her face. "Daniel."

He wanted to touch her, say something very important.

"You're going."

"Yes."

"Where?"

"I don't know yet."

"What will you do?"

"I don't know that yet either. Who knows, I might sing again one day."

"That would be good." He winced inwardly.

"Take care of yourself, Daniel."

"I will. And you. You look after yourself."

"Goodbye, then."

"Goodbye. Wait! How will I know where you are? That you're OK?"

"I'll send you a postcard," she smiled as she picked up her case.

"Yes – but after that?"

"I'll send you another postcard."

From behind them came the roar of a car engine. They both looked round as a silver Mercedes swerved past the tourist coaches and headed straight for them, very fast. There was a screech of brakes and the slam of a car door. Kamal Sharif, immaculate in a cream linen suit and pale green silk shirt, stood by his car, his dark eyes fixed on Rachel. So this was how it was going to end, thought Daniel, miserably. There could be no escape, however hard one tried. There must be something he could do for Rachel. He was paralysed with indecision.

Kamal put his hand inside his jacket. Oh my God! thought Daniel. Then out of the pocket he pulled an iridescent silk scarf. It shone like the rainbows that daily, now, lit up the skies. He placed it gently round Rachel's neck. Daniel watched, transfixed, as Kamal adjusted the scarf slightly. He saw Rachel's eyes close for a moment as the fine fingers brushed against her pale neck. Then Kamal got back into the car and drove off. Rachel hesitated for a moment, then continued her journey towards the departure lounge.

"What was all that about?" Patrick asked as he caught up with Daniel.

"I don't know. Mutual forgiveness? A token of some kind of love? An apology?"

"You're being a bit deep for me."

"If only. Just as confused as ever."

"Well, that's good. Look – there's the plane. It's landing now. I hate that bit, where you don't know if the pilot's going to remember to lower the wheels. There! It's down. Thank God for that."

The aeroplane came to a standstill on the runway. The door opened and a small truck propelled the steps towards it. Daniel and Patrick walked over to the high chain-link fence and peered through it at the descending passengers.

"There she is! Isabel! Here! Over here! Look, Daniel, – there – just behind that woman in the hat."

Daniel could see her now. She was returning Patrick's wave as she walked down the steep steps to the tarmac. A tall fair man was holding her elbow as she negotiated her descent.

"Typical Izzy!" Patrick grinned. "Can always be relied on to find a good-looking young man to hold her hand. She's only pretending to need help, you know. She could skip down those steps in seconds if she wanted to, eh, Daniel? Are you all right? I'm going to meet Isabel as she comes through immigration. See you in a minute."

Daniel watched, paralysed, as the tall, fair-haired man let go of Isabel's arm, then veered away from the procession of disembarking travellers, and walked purposefully towards him. Daniel felt his throat constrict. He raised his shaking hands and gripped the fence. He felt familiar long fingers tightening around his own. Daniel rested his head against the fence and closed his eyes.

"Surprise!" said Jonathan, quietly.

Brighton, August 4th 2000

POST CARD

THE ADDRESS TO BE WRITTEN ON THIS SIDE

Invitation to a concert
September 27th 2000
7.30 pm
St Bartholomew's Church
Ann St
Brighton

R x

Daniel Maddalison
FCO London
c/o King Charles St.
London SW1A 2AH

EPILOGUE
September 27th 2000

A turquoise and white taxi speeds away from the railway station, then comes to a standstill. The driver glances in the mirror and sees a stressed-looking man in his mid-thirties. One of those London types, no question about it.

"Probably been just as quick to walk, you know. Bloody new road layout – if they'd bothered to consult us cabbies instead of paying a lot of so-called transport consultants, we'd all get home a lot sooner. Sorry about all this. Look, I'll drop you here and you can cut through that road over there. You can't miss it. Bloody great monstrosity. That's four pounds exactly."

"Here. Keep the change."

"Thanks, mate. Have a good evening, now."

As he shuts the taxi door, his mobile phone beeps. He checks the message. It is from Jonathan.

Missed exit from M23. Sorry. See you in there x

Daniel Maddison smiles as he switches off the phone and pushes open the massive wooden door of the church. He rummages in his pocket for his wallet, knocking over a plastic stand of Christian Aid leaflets as he does so.

"Shh!" hisses a woman sitting behind a desk. "You'll have to wait until this piece's finished. That's two pounds. And here's a programme."

He picks up the leaflets, then glances at a multicoloured poster advertising a fund-raising concert for Africa. A child's sun extends its golden rays towards a smiling lion and a slightly stunted giraffe. He hears muffled applause.

"Right, now, creep in round the side. I think there are a few seats towards the front. Here, don't forget your programme."

The woman opens the door to let him through. He walks quickly up the side aisle as rows of children file back to their pews, grinning and peering into the audience to find their parents. Other children, slightly older, take their places at the front of the nave. Some are carrying African drums and beaters, others are holding thin wooden tubes that rattle slightly as they steady them.

Two boys, aged about nine or ten, step forward. Very carefully, they invert their tubes. A thousand tiny metal beads cascade through each tube. They turn them again. The rainstorm swells, then dies away. The rest of the choir takes a deep breath. A humming sound fills the church. A single plaintive note. Then a slight, dark-haired girl takes a step forward from the body of the choir and stands between the two boys. Her dark blue eyes shine with excitement as she looks confidently out at the rows of faces.

"Had I the heavens' embroidered cloths enwrought with golden and silver light," she sings out in a sweet, clear voice.

Daniel's hands tighten on the programme. His eyes scan the rows of names. A rushing sound in his ears drowns out her voice for a few seconds. When he looks up again, the familiar rhythm has changed. The drums come in softly, followed by the beaters. Then the rest of the choir joins in. "Of night and light and the half-light," they sing, again and again as the drums become louder and louder, then stop abruptly. Then, as if an echo, the child sings the first line of the song again. Sings it time and time again, becoming quieter and quieter each time, until there is silence. The boys tip their rain sticks one last time. The audience erupts into applause. First the girl, then the two boys, then the rest of the choir bows. Daniel wants to clap but his hands are shaking too much.

He scans the audience. It does not take long to find her. She is sitting in the front row. Dressed in kingfisher blue. Pushing her fair hair away from her face as she smiles up at her daughter who takes a last dignified bow then walks back to her seat, touching her mother's hand as she passes.

———— • ————

Acknowledgements

Thanks to Candida Lacey, Corinne Pearlman,
Jannet King, Nancy Webber and all at Myriad Editions.

Thanks for all their support and encouragement to
Umi Sinha, Alastair Burtt, Sian James, Cynthia Stirrup,
Lindsay Davies, Sally O'Reilly, Bobbie Farsides, Jackie
Wills, Steve Fish, Anthony Mahony; to my children,
Anna and Sebastian, and to my mother, Maria Eckstein.

Special thanks to Anna Burtt for the postcards.

The novel was started during a creative writing course
at the University of Sussex and, while it was inspired
by my time working in West Africa, all events and
characters are fictitious.

"Thomson skilfully evokes the era and the slow-moving quality of childhood summers, suggesting the menace lurking just beyond the vision of her young protagonists. A study of memory and guilt with several twists." *Guardian*

"This emotionally charged thriller grips from the first paragraph, and a nail-biting level of suspense is maintained throughout. A great second novel." *She*

"Such is the vividness of the descriptions of the location in this well structured and well written novel that I want to get the next train down. On the edge of my seat? No way – I was cowering under it."
www.shotsmag.co.uk

Price: £6.99
ISBN: 978-0-9549309-4-3

"An exquisitely crafted début novel set in a post-apocalyptic landscape. I'm rationing myself to five pages per day in order to make it last."
Guardian Unlimited

"An all-too-convincing picture of life in the rural Midlands in the middle of this century – cold and stormy, with most modern conveniences long-since gone, and with small, mainly self-sufficient, communities struggling to maintain a degree of social order. It is very atmospheric and certainly leaves an indelible imprint on the psyche."
BBC Radio 4 Open Book

"A decidedly original tale. Psychologically sophisticated, it demands our attention. Ignore it, O Philistines, at your peril."
www.bookgroup.info

Price: £6.99
ISBN: 978-0-9549309-2-9

MORE FROM MYRIAD EDITIONS

This celebration of Brighton and Brightonians – resident, itinerant and visiting – is a feast of words and pictures specially commissioned from established artists and emerging talents.

"*The Brighton Book* is a fantastic idea and I loved writing a piece with crazy wonderful Brighton as the theme. Everybody should buy the book because it's such a great mix of energy and ideas."
Jeanette Winterson

"Packed with unique perspectives on the city...
The Brighton Book has hedonism at its heart. Give a man a fish and you'll feed him for a day. Give him *The Brighton Book* and you will feed him for a lifetime." *Argus*

Contributors include Melissa Benn, Louis de Bernières, Piers Gough, Roy Greenslade, Bonnie Greer, Lee Harwood, Mick Jackson, Lenny Kaye, Nigella Lawson, Martine McDonagh, Boris Mikhailov, Woodrow Phoenix, John Riddy, Meg Rosoff, Miranda Sawyer, Posy Simmonds, Ali Smith, Catherine Smith, Diana Souhami, Lesley Thomson and Jeanette Winterson.

Price: £9.99
ISBN: 978-0-9549309-0-5